The Captain's Daughter

THE CAPTAIN'S DAUGHTER

By ELIZABETH COATSWORTH

Decorations by Ralph Ray

THE MACMILLAN COMPANY · NEW YORK

[*1950*]

Contents

The Captain's Daughter

CHAPTER I

Janet and Alan

FROM where she stood by the window at the end of the up-stairs hall, Janet Pierce could watch Alan harnessing the new horse. Looked at from above, the scene was laid out almost like an embroidery pattern of green lawns divided by a white picket fence, with the brown, square, rather shabby-looking house next door, the drive, on which lay a drift of fallen horse chestnut blossoms from the trees which lined it, and in front of the square brown stable, the figure which was the focus of Janet's deep attention—Alan Loring harnessing the new horse.

She had often noticed how well Alan did things with his hands. The horse was a black mare, high-strung and fidgety, stamping and tossing its head in impatience, but Alan took his unhurried time. She watched his hands lifting the harness into place, fastening the buckles. When his back was turned, she watched the set of his shoulders and the line of his neck and the way his brown hair swirled at the crown of his head. Sometimes she had to move a little so as not to lose sight of him behind a cluster of chestnut leaves. When he turned, she caught her breath. Would he look up and see her at the window? For a moment she drew back, as she would have done two weeks ago; then, smiling, she pressed to the pane, ready to wave if he should look up after all. She needn't be ashamed now if Alan caught her watching him. But when he didn't glance up, she was satisfied to study his unconscious face. She loved the set of his chin, the big half-smiling mouth, the balanced nose and brow and eyes. He was almost too handsome to be true. Janet shut her eyes. But when she opened them again, Alan was as handsome as ever.

Now he wheeled up the light democrat, slipped the thills into place, fastened the traces, and unhitched the black mare's head. As he led the horse in a half circle to face the street, Janet tapped on the window as a signal of readiness, which went unheard in the crunch of wheels on gravel.

Now Alan jumped into the carriage, there was a flash of sunlight whirling along the spokes, a shine from the polished sides of the mare, and the beat of hoofs. Whatever else might be shabby on the Loring premises, it was never their horse nor their carriage, nor their own street clothes, for that matter.

"I'm coming!"

Janet turned and, catching her wide skirts up from her feet, ran down the hall towards the stairs. She had lingered too long already for the joy of watching Alan. She would be late at the door when he drove up and she had meant to be there waiting for him.

But as she tore down the stairs, Mrs. Pierce came out of the parlor, lifting one hand in a gesture of reproof.

"Janet dear, whatever it is, it will keep."

Janet cried gaily, over her shoulder, "No, it won't, Mother! It's Alan and the new horse!"

"Be back by twelve."

But by this time Janet was already out of the door and probably did not hear.

"I don't believe that her father would approve of the way Janet's behaving," Mrs. Pierce thought, her face looking rather tired as she went back to her desk and the month's accounts. Outside, she heard the horse start off with a spurt of speed, leaping forward the moment Janet was seated, perhaps before. Why hadn't Janet told her earlier that she was going driving with Alan? And where were they going and when would they be back? Of course they had known Alan since he was a child. But Captain Pierce might not approve of the young people's seeing so much of one another. He had never cared for the Lorings. "All looks and no spunk," he used to say about the father.

It was hard to have to make so many decisions with the Captain always away. Lydia had never caused her any worry and now she was married to Jo Loomis and lived near Boston. Whenever Mrs. Pierce thought of Lydia, she was filled with the glow of accomplishment. There was one child of whom she might be proud without reservation. Not that Lydia was as beautiful as Janet, but she was pretty enough and always so well mannered and sensible. Not headstrong like Janet, nor sulky like Stephen. You couldn't speak to Stephen nowadays without having that impatient look come across his face. He wasn't disobedient exactly but he was always getting off by himself and glowering at everyone. Even with the little children, lots of problems came up where Mrs. Pierce missed the Captain's advice. Take that time last winter when Ted was sick and she had been forced to make up her mind whether or not to send to Portland for Dr. Maynard. After she had sent for him, it seemed unnecessary, and twenty-five dollars was a lot of money. Then ought she to have taken Deborah away from Mrs. Digby's school just because one morning she had come early to fetch the child and had found Mrs. Digby, with her hair combed down over her face, sitting at her desk watching the children like a tiger in a jungle?

Deborah had never mentioned anything about Mrs. Digby's hair at home. She was so little that she thought all teachers combed their hair over their faces.

"You never can tell whether she's awake or asleep," explained Deborah as they walked home together. "You can't tell when she's watching you."

It didn't seem nice to Mrs. Pierce. She had not allowed Deborah to go back to Mrs. Digby, and instead was giving her lessons at home. But Deborah was often idle and the lessons made one more drain on Mrs. Pierce's time, always in arrears. When she got up each morning, the day seemed to lie so long before her like a piece of new cloth, but right away it began to shrink and pucker, and by the time she got to bed again that night, her day was all in shreds behind her.

If only Captain Pierce were home more often, he would make the decisions. He liked to make decisions as much as she hated to make them. All the children—yes, even Stephen in a queer way—were like her except Janet. They were glad to be told what to do.

But Janet was her father's daughter.

Mrs. Pierce considered her headstrong child and felt vaguely alarmed. In the last letter they had received from the Captain, he had said that they might expect him home in May. It was late May now, but still they had heard nothing further. For once Mrs. Pierce was not sure that she looked forward to her husband's return. Suppose he disapproved of Janet and Alan?

"But she's so pretty and so charming," she comforted herself. "She'll manage her father." Captain Pierce had thoroughly approved of Lydia's marriage. And Alan was a dear boy and the handsomest human being she had ever laid eyes on, unless one counted Janet. That they should be drawn towards one another seemed as inevitable as that the sun should rise.

But was that the way the Captain would look at it?

Sighing a little, Mrs. Pierce bent again over the ledger. She wouldn't borrow trouble. There was always enough and to spare at one's feet.

"Are you glad to see me?" demanded Janet settling into her seat beside Alan as the horse leaped forward.

Alan glanced at her sideways.

"I'll show you when we're out of town."

Something in Janet went weak. Until a few days ago she had never been kissed. Oh, a quick smack on the cheek or the chin as she turned away her head in a game of Drop-the-Handkerchief or Post Office, but never a kiss which meant anything, where lips meet lips and heart reaches out to heart. It seemed to her that the village was almost unbearably beautiful this morning. The houses looked so clean in their green yards as they whirled past; the leaves on the trees had not quite lost their flowery appearance; and the smell of lilacs was part of the air which she breathed, along with a pleasant odor of soaped leather and well-curried horse.

It was all so almost painfully beautiful that Janet's eyes fastened with something like relief on the broad figure of

[5]

Florence Andrews coming along the sidewalk. As usual, Florence was overdressed. Her bright unsuitable silk and double gold chain at once proclaimed her the banker's daughter and made her face look more sallow and her eyes more squinting than ever.

"There's Flowery Flo," whispered Janet. Alan glanced up.

"Hello, Alan!" Florence called, waving vigorously. She ignored Janet, though they had sat next to one another at school for two years and went to all the same parties. Janet sketched an airy bow. Her dimple was showing.

"See you tonight," bawled Florence above the noise of the carriage and still as though Janet were invisible.

Janet laughed as they drove on. She felt Alan's shoulder against hers, leaning towards her by the merest fraction of a motion. For one second his hand rested on her hands folded on her lap. She felt his strength even in that passing touch. From her protected tower of love, she looked out serenely. She didn't even ask what Florence meant by, "See you tonight," but Alan explained:

"She got me cornered yesterday when I was downtown and I didn't know how to get out of it, Jan."

"Poor Alan."

"If you want me to, I'll tell her I can't come."

"It's too late now." Janet thought, "I'm sure we'd talked about his coming over this evening. How funny! But we can't be together all the time, I suppose. It doesn't matter." She was ready to drop the subject but Alan couldn't let it alone.

"She's the homeliest girl in town and bold as brass," he went on, almost uneasily.

"What does it matter?" Janet asked. They weren't quite

[6]

out of town, but she felt his arm go about her waist and his touch seemed like a wall built about her to keep all sorrow away from her forever. No one but a cat was in sight and, careless of who might be in the windows behind the curtains, Janet leaned her head on Alan's shoulder. Weren't they engaged to be married?

The horse fled on before them, spurning the ground under its swift hoofs, and above an empty field a bobolink hung in the air, singing and singing.

Now there were only farms about them, with cows and sheep, with plowed lands and woodlands.

Alan pulled the horse down to a walk and his arm tightened about Janet.

CHAPTER II

The Captain Returns

Mrs. Pierce was marking sheets and pillowcases from the pile of linen which she had brought into the dining room. She was glad to be alone, quietly at work. The morning sunlight made two slanting pillars between the heavy draperies at the windows, and one fell across the stove, throwing its iron scrolls into high relief and shining brightly on the cheek and curls of the small iron child which served as a handle to the lid.

The portrait of Deborah Pierce above the mantel of the bricked-in fireplace was in shadow, but even in shadow it drew the eye, and more than once Mrs. Pierce glanced up as though she felt the presence of another person in the room.

Deborah Pierce had died when her son, the Captain, was a boy. This portrait had been painted before her marriage. It showed a girl, with reddish-brown hair arranged in a Grecian knot, wearing a wide sleeved, green gown, cut low in the neck. An India scarf was caught about the elbows. The artist had not been remarkable in his handling of materials and background, but he had succeeded in giving to the girl's face a look of singular joyousness and youth. There was a trace of obstinacy in the line of the chin, per-

[8]

haps a headstrong light in the gray-green eyes, but the open generous expression of the whole beautiful face more than offset this suggestion of wilfulness. Here had been someone eager to give back to life the bounty which life had given to her in such overflowing measure. Here was a heart ready to love and to trust, and it was characteristic of Deborah that she had chosen to have painted in her hand an envelope, addressed "To my own true love" (as one might read by turning one's head a little sideways), instead of the more usual rose or book of devotion. But then, the picture had been painted for her affianced husband to hang in his cabin, for he, like his son after him, was a captain in the China trade.

When Janet was born, her father had been somewhat comforted for the baby's being another daughter by her unmistakable likeness to the portrait of her grandmother.

"She's a Pierce," he declared, adding, "but she'll never be as handsome as Mother."

For several years the likeness had persisted, and then it had disappeared. By that time, however, Janet was very deeply installed in her father's affections. They were much alike in their tastes and ways, so much that Mrs. Pierce believed that Janet remained her father's favorite even after Stephen came and little Ted, who weren't Pierces at all except in name.

Thinking of her family, Mrs. Pierce wondered where they all were, leaving the house so empty behind them. The boys, of course, were at school and Deborah had gone to market with the cook, Minnie. Janet was up early and off to the house of her friend, Susan Mann, for an all-day quilting bee. All the girls would be there. They were finishing a friendship quilt for Betsey Prince, who was to be married

[9]

next week. Mrs. Pierce's mind veered a little as the wind of marriage blew upon it. Captain Pierce had been away ever since Lydia's wedding, nearly two years ago. When he left home, Stephen was as good-natured as a puppy and Janet was a schoolgirl without a serious thought in her head. Now she was just beginning to look like her grandmother again. When he came back, he would be startled by the likeness. The painting over the mantel might be Janet's portrait in fancy dress, even to the high carriage of the head on the long neck and the warm loving look at the eyes and the obstinate set of the lips. It was Janet's being in love that had made the likeness complete. Mrs. Pierce had noticed it one morning at breakfast.

"What's happened to you, Janet?" she had asked, and without more ado Janet had cried:

"I'm in love."

Captain Pierce would certainly approve of the likeness, but would he approve of its cause? He was not a man to discuss his neighbors, but Mrs. Pierce knew that he had a kindly contempt for Mr. Hiram Loring. Surely, that need not extend to his son? Alan was a young man with excellent manners and was well connected through both his father and mother. The Lorings weren't poor, exactly. Annie Downer had brought her husband a very good fortune and he had inherited something from his mother as well. From his mother. For a moment a thought half formed in Mrs. Pierce's mind, but she would not allow it to take actual shape. There was a sound on the steps going up to the verandah, and she rose, pushing her work from her.

"Minnie and Deborah are back early," she thought, going rather unnecessarily to meet them at the door, but it was a boy, whom she found waiting, with a telegram.

After all these years of being a captain's wife, her heart still beat heavily whenever a telegram arrived. She knew that this would almost certainly be from the owners saying that the *Phoenix* had been sighted, but still the possibility of some unexpected disaster made her hand tremble and her face whiten. When she married, she had married suspense as well as a husband, so that she would never again hear the wind in the chimney without thinking of sails at sea, nor receive sudden news without a mounting terror.

As soon as she had thanked the boy and closed the door, Mrs. Pierce tore open the envelope and read the telegram at a glance. There was no disaster here. The *Phoenix* had been sighted and should be in Boston by that afternoon. Captain Pierce might be expected next day on the afternoon train. One more voyage was over. Once more Captain Pierce would sleep safe under his own roof. And in the flood of relief and happiness, Mrs. Pierce forgot all about Janet's affairs and Stephen's difficulties and only thought of favorite dishes to be prepared, of a new dress of her own to be pressed and of a telegram to Lydia, who might be able to see her father in Boston.

Debby could scarcely remember the Captain. "He's that big man in the picture," she said, "the one with brass buttons," but she knew well enough that it was from him that her Japanese doll with the slanting eyes had come and her set of dolls' teacups from China. And Ted could remember, oh, clearly he remembered a walk he had taken with his father, during which they had come upon two dogs fighting and how his father had kicked them apart. He,

Ted, had been terrified by the snarling and scrambling and blood, but his father had separated the dogs as matter-of-factly as he would have buttered a piece of bread.

It was hard to be sure what Stephen felt. Perhaps he didn't know himself. Janet was delighted.

"Won't he be pleased about Alan and me?" she cried, catching her mother in her arms and waltzing her about for a few steps. "Oh, won't he be pleased, Mother, to know that I'm going to marry the nicest young man in all the world?"

"Fudge," said Stephen, "you girls are all alike."

Laughing and panting, Mrs. Pierce pushed Janet away and settled her dress in order. "Don't tell your father right off," she said. "Wait until he's been home a little, dear, and I've had a chance to prepare him."

"But I want to surprise him! Think what fun to be able to say 'You are now being kissed by the future Mrs. Alan Loring, Father.'"

"Oh, no, no, dear. That would be too much of a surprise. Trust me. Don't speak of it until Father's been home a few days. It's much wiser. Men don't like to be told things too suddenly. And Ted and Debby, you listen to me, both of you. If either of you mentions Alan's name I'll spat your hands for you. Do you understand? And you won't say anything, will you, Stephen dear?"

Stephen shook his head, as though he couldn't bring himself to take any further part in the discussion, and went out, grinning derisively. "You wait until you're in love!" Janet called after him.

"It'll be a long wait," he muttered, more to himself than to her.

Next afternoon, the family hired the town hack and

drove to the station to meet the Boston train, which arrived only ten minutes late. Captain Pierce descended amid a deluge of mysteriously shaped bundles wrapped in fine matting and teakwood trunks with brass handles. His homecomings paled any arrival of Santa Claus into insignificance. He looked well, and as masterful and handsome as ever. To see him with his wife on one arm and Janet on the other, with Stephen following with some of the luggage and the younger children running ahead as they swept down the station platform was to see a very charming portrait of a fine family.

That afternoon, the parlor was littered with opened parcels and half unpacked boxes. Mrs. Pierce and Janet went about delightedly trying on embroidered shawls or fingering china and tortoiseshell, and even Stephen stayed home, instead of going to see his friend, Millard, and showed something approaching enthusiasm for a Chinese god and a Samurai sword which his father had brought him.

"You spoil us," said Mrs. Pierce coming to sit beside her husband on the sofa.

"I like to," the Captain returned with an affectionate laugh.

Janet at that moment turned towards them, as though about to speak, but her mother shook her head and the girl picked up again the mandarin robe she was about to try on, in a moment displaying her neat bodice and billowing skirts encircled with dragons and clouds.

"Have you noticed how much Janet looks like her grandmother?" Captain Pierce remarked in tones not intended for his daughter's ears, but which she could not help overhearing.

It was in a mood of family unity and content that the

Pierces sat down that evening to their dinner of thick soup followed by a great roast of beef, flanked by Yorkshire pudding, with dishes of vegetables, and plates of hot rolls and saucers of welcoming jellies and relishes. There were so many questions to be asked about the voyage and so many things to be told about affairs in Thomaston that it was late before Norah cleared the table for dessert.

Janet rose.

"Excuse me, Father," she said. "I hate to leave, but there's a spelling bee this evening and I'm the leader of one of the teams and I don't know how to get out of it very well."

"Of course not, Daughter," Captain Pierce replied heartily. "We have plenty of time ahead of us. Come, give me a kiss and run along. Who's going to see you home?"

"Oh, Alan, I guess."

Debby remarked, "Alan always sees Janet home."

Even this might have passed if Ted had not shrieked, "Tattle-tale-spoil-sport! You know Mama is going to smack your hands for that."

Debby burst into a loud flood of excuses and explanations.

"Children! Children! Be still this minute!" poor Mrs. Pierce cried. "You will have to leave the table!"

Captain Pierce said, "Leave the table, both of you, and go to your rooms and stay there. Would you mind going, too, Stephen? And tell Norah she is not required in the dining room until the bell is rung. Shut the door behind you when you go out, please."

"Is it all right for me to go over to Millard's?" Stephen asked.

His father nodded curtly. There was silence until the

children had left the room, followed by Stephen, who drew the sliding doors into place, giving Janet a glance in which a dark superiority was not untouched with pity.

When the doors were closed the Captain turned to his daughter, still standing near her chair, frozen in her place.

"Sit down, Janet."

Janet sat down.

"John, I saw no harm," Mrs. Pierce began breathlessly, but the Captain silenced her by a shake of the head, his eyes still on his daughter.

"Now tell me what this means, Janet."

Janet's head went up and she looked directly at her father.

"It means that Alan and I are in love and that we're going to be married."

"So that's what's been going on." Captain Pierce's voice was heavy. "Well, you're both young. This affair stops here. Do you understand, Janet? And you needn't look as though your heart were breaking. Puppy love doesn't break hearts. I should have foreseen this and have left explicit orders that you were not to be on any terms of intimacy with the Lorings, but I thought my attitude towards that family was sufficiently well understood."

"And what is wrong with Alan, Father?"

"He's a chip of the old block. All the family is good-looking and worthless. I've known his father and uncles since I was a boy. I knew his grandfather before him and his great-uncles and I know the history of his great grand-father, who was another Alan. Every one of them has been good-looking and not a one of them has amounted to a hill of beans. If they get a position through their in-laws, they can't hold it for six months. They aren't bad men, they

[15]

don't beat their wives, they don't drink, they don't steal. But they're just good for nothing in this world but to marry a girl with money and take things easy for the rest of their lives. And you, Janet, aren't going to be the wife Alan Loring marries and, by gravy! my money isn't going to be the money Alan Loring spends!"

Janet's face was white and her eyes were wide open and blind but her voice was still low.

"You aren't fair, Father. Alan can't be judged by his father. His Uncle Sam's working in the bank now. And Alan's got his mother's family in him, too. His grandfather Downer was a captain and a friend of Grandfather Pierce's. You have the watch he gave Grandfather after Grandfather rescued him and every member of his crew when the *Three Sisters* was wrecked."

"You are right, Janet. And in any other family I should count the mother's blood. But the Loring strain is strong and they breed true to one type. Whoever they marry, and they marry well, when the sons come along they are lazy Lorings down to the last man-jack of them. You spoke of Sam. I'll bet he'll be out of the bank before the Fourth of July. But to hold to Alan. Has he a job, Janet?"

"Not yet. He's going to get one in the fall."

"That's what I say. The Lorings are always going to get jobs. But they usually get married first, and then they don't need to. It's a lot easier to put your arm around a pretty girl's waist than to buckle down to ten hours a day of hard work."

Janet was trembling.

"Father, that isn't fair. You scarcely know Alan and I've known him all my life. And I *love* him. I understand

[16]

him. We've often talked about the kind of work he wants to do, often and often—"

The Captain's voice broke in, irresistible as a ground-swell after a storm.

"And it will never get beyond talk. You're a young girl and know little of the world. You must take my advice—"

"But Mother likes Alan—"

"Yes, John, he seems—"

"Seems! Seems! That's the trouble. He seems all that a young man should be, but I know there's nothing behind his seeming. I could give you the history of the family—I sailed as second mate when Hiram's brother, Alexander, was first mate. I've lived next to Hiram for twenty years. No, no. You can't teach a Loring new tricks. I know them one and all—"

This time it was Janet who broke in.

"But Alan is Alan, and I should love him if every one of his family was in jail or the poorhouse!"

"No doubt you would, like many a little fool before you. But not a red cent of my money shall ever go into Alan Loring's pocket, do you hear me, Janet? I am your father and I shall waste no more time arguing with you. Either you will go to the bee and give me your promise to come home with someone else, or you will march up to your room and stay there."

Without a word, Janet pushed back her chair from the table and walked out of the room.

Her mother started to follow her.

"Oh, Janet dear, please do what your father—" she began, but Captain Pierce laid his hand on her arm.

[17]

"She must make up her own mind, Adelaide," he said and leaving his wife in tears followed Janet up the stairs to her own room, where she stood in the darkness, a faint shape against the dusk-lighted windows.

"Janet," her father said slowly, "I am not acting in anger but for your own protection. Give me your promise and you may go as you planned."

There was no answer and no motion from the figure at the window, and after a moment Captain Pierce took the key from the inside of the lock and quietly closed the door, locked it and pocketed the key.

Only after his firm tread had receded along the hallway and down the stairs did Janet turn and, running to her bed, throw herself upon it, sobbing. What, oh, what had happened to her beautiful day, to all the joy of the homecoming, to her happy love? Next to Alan she loved her father more than anyone on earth, and now he was trying to destroy her happiness, to make her despise her future husband and to betray him.

"It's not true, darling, I don't believe any of it," she sobbed into her pillow. "Your father isn't well, I know he isn't, but you're strong and ambitious. You've told me, again and again, what you're planning to do. How *can* Father say such poisonous things? It's like trying to kill something, trying to kill our love."

For awhile, Janet lay, easing the strain and shock of the last half hour. Why, Father had scarcely scolded her before in all her life, and now he didn't care how miserable he made her. Why hadn't he made a fuss when Lydia and Jo got married? She had heard it said that captains were hard men and she saw that even her father could be as hard as stone. Well, she was his daughter. She would be as hard as

he was, if necessary. Nothing and no one should come between her and her love. It was the most beautiful thing she
had ever dreamed of, like sunlight, and like things growing,
and like the pause in church before the organ begins, and
like rest when you are tired and like wind blowing white
clouds. It was joy and she would cling to it and trust to it
or she would not be worthy of it. She would know neither
doubt nor fear but only love, but only love.

It is possible that Janet fell asleep for a few minutes, a
short swooning sleep of physical and emotional exhaustion,
but when she became conscious her eyes were dry and she
felt much calmer.

She got up and walked again to the window. The last
broken strips of sunset had paled, but in the green sky a
moon, almost at the full, confronted her. It was not the silver
moon of romance but a very disproportionately large yellow moon, like a balloon or a lighted Japanese lantern
swinging upon a star. Its light mingled with the with-
drawing day to show her the scene below quite clearly.
The lawn did not look distant, and just beyond the lawn
lay the empty sidewalk and the street and freedom. She
hoped that Stephen wouldn't come back when he was least
wanted. Nowadays it was hard to tell what Stephen would
do.

She looked at the Loring house. Alan's room was dark.
He had probably gone to the Driscolls' already. The young
people usually gathered in a hit-or-miss way at the bees and
then paired off for the walk home, frequently taken in a
most round-about fashion. As theirs would have been. As
it would be.

Quietly, Janet went to her dressing table and without
lighting her candle brushed and combed her hair and

straightened her dress. Then she opened one of the windows and, taking firm hold of the trumpet vine outside, stood on the sill, trying to find some footing among the twisted stems, and so swung off into space. The main strand of the vine was as thick as her arm and securely fastened to the side of the house, but the smaller stems kept breaking under her feet and, by the time she reached the ground, the palms of her hands were red and scraped and her dress was torn. She had used that ladder more than once as a little girl, but she was lighter and more muscular then. Now at least, she was there on the ground and that was all Janet cared about. There had been no sign of Stephen, or of anyone else. She had been lucky. Walking on the grass, rather than on the gravel of the drive, she slipped past the windows of the room where her father and mother sat with the children and hurried off under the rising and shining moon.

CHAPTER III

Let's Get Married Tonight

THERE was a rap on Janet's door.

"Janet," came her father's voice, "Janet."

When there was no answer from within, Captain Pierce stepped back and saw only darkness along the still.

"Janet, have you gone to sleep?"

Still no answer.

The Captain turned away and went downstairs to rejoin his wife.

"She's sulky," he said. "She won't answer."

Mrs. Pierce looked more troubled than ever, started to say something and thought better of it. The Captain had not reproached her, but she now reproached herself. If only at the very beginning, say that first time when Janet and Alan had sat on the steps singing,

"Down in the valley
Where the green grass grows
There sat Janet (Alan's voice)
Sweet as a rose,
She sang, she sang,
She sang so sweet;
Along came Alan (Janet's voice)
And kissed her on the cheek."

That was when she should have hurried out and have sent him straight home. But wasn't the mischief done already? Hadn't that mysterious air of being in bloom already fallen upon Janet? But now this conflict between those she loved oppressed her, and she could feel the weight of her heart actually heavy in her bosom. She drew a chair beside her husband's, where he sat looking before him, and laid her hand rather timidly on his.

"I'm so sorry, John," she ventured. "And on your first night home."

He roused at that.

"Adelaide, my dear, don't be upset. These things happen in most families. I wish that I might let the matter pass, but I cannot reconcile it with my conscience. Come. Stephen's in and gone to bed half an hour ago. We might as well go to bed, too, and take counsel in sleep. We can do no good moping here."

The lights were turned out and together Captain and Mrs. Pierce climbed the stairs, lighted by the moonlight which shone white from the window on the landing. The lilacs were in bloom and the smell of lilacs came even into the house, the very breath of spring and of young love.

Mrs. Pierce whispered over her shoulder, "John, may I say good night to Janet?"

Her husband nodded and went into their room, while she knocked softly at her daughter's door.

"Janet, Janet, I want to say good night to you, dear."

There was no answer.

Mrs. Pierce knew what Captain Pierce could not know, that Janet was a light sleeper, waking very quickly at any sound.

"Janet," she called more insistently, and when no answer came, she rapped hard on the door and called, "Janet! Janet!" in a frightened voice. Debby woke up in the next room and began whimpering, Stephen stuck his head out of his door, looking indignant at being wakened, and Captain Pierce came into the hall.

"Calm yourself, Adelaide, calm yourself, and you others, go back to bed." Then he added to his wife in a lower voice, "You will only encourage Janet in her disobedience."

But Mrs. Pierce continued to press at the door, crying, "Hurry, John! Open it! Something's happened to Janet!"

Before her insistence, the Captain drew out the key, and unlocked the door and followed his wife into Janet's room. Whatever she may have feared to find was not there, but only the orderly moonlit chamber, with the bed a little disarranged and the breeze coming in through the open window, stirring the pale ruffles of the curtains.

Captain Pierce went to the window and stuck his head out. He saw the vine, which grew heavy as a young tree along the side of the house, and on the grass the dark untidiness of sprays broken off and fallen to the roots.

He drew his head in and faced his wife.

"Janet's gone to the spelling bee," he announced calmly. "Now, Adelaide, you've had a tiring day. Go to bed. I have a letter to write."

"You're going to sit up for her, John."

"Probably. But you need not be afraid that I am angry at being disobeyed. I should be if she had deceived me, but she gave me fair warning that she would go if she could. Don't worry. I shall do what I believe must be done, but nothing more."

And with his arm about his wife's waist, Captain Pierce led her from Janet's quiet empty room, and the breeze, finding the open door, strengthened and, first swaying it a little to and fro, finally closed it with a bang which shook the house.

The spelling bee at the Driscolls' was off to a good start. Mr. Driscoll ran a successful grain and feed store and his wife, Nettie, had taught school before she married. They both liked to have the house filled with young people, really more than did their girls, who were at a somewhat awkward age and were rather shy. But Mr. Driscoll's hearty voice could be heard greeting every newcomer with a joke and a slap on the shoulder for each of the young men and a compliment for each of the girls, and Mrs. Driscoll came in and out from the kitchen, smiling and wiping the steam from her glasses. The double doors between the dining room and parlor had been opened and the dining room table pushed back to make more room for the party, which as usual broke up into busily talking clusters. When everyone had arrived except Janet, there was some talk of Alan's going to find out if she were coming, but nothing came of it. Flo suggested that she could do the choosing as well as Janet, and without waiting for much agreement, chose Alan as first on her team.

Just then Janet arrived amid a hubbub of welcome.

"Come in! Come in, Jan! We were afraid you weren't coming. We thought perhaps with the Captain just home—"

"Oh, no," said Janet. "Father's coming won't make me change any of my plans."

There was a defiance in her voice which no one noticed

or recognized. May, hurrying forward to welcome her, exclaimed, "Mercy sakes, Jan, what have you done to your hands?"

"Oh, nothing, I caught my dress on a paling of the Daniels' fence and fell. I was hurrying. But it doesn't matter a bit. Where's Alan?"

Janet looked about the room, her eyes searching frankly for Alan. It happened that she had never told a lie before in her life. This to May was her first, and it was told to protect her father. If there was to be war between them it should be, so far as she could manage, a private war. Janet had no desire for the sympathy of her friends. All she wanted was to be with Alan and in his presence to wipe out forever the memory of all that her father had said.

Just at that moment, Flo Andrews called from the back of the room, "Let's go on choosing, May. You were late, Janet, so I'm leader," and as Flo moved forward a little, Janet caught a glimpse of Alan behind her, looking towards her with a welcoming smile.

She swept in upon that corner of the room.

"Nonsense, Flo, I'm not very late," and everyone backed Janet up:

"We've just begun."—"Flo's only chosen Alan so far."—"We'll begin again."

Janet's serenity that evening was profoundly disturbed by the quarrel with her father, and she did not take Flo's poaching with the calm she had felt a few days before. And Alan? But she could not criticize Alan. Hadn't he said that Flo was bold as brass? He couldn't very well push past a girl as solid as Flo to join her at the door. Of course he couldn't!

And with a brilliant smile she chose Alan first for her team.

It was a curious evening. Janet was like a person in a fever, her eyes brighter, her cheeks redder and her laugh quicker than it had ever been. Her excitement, held back, burned fiercely, and she shone and glowed in its inner flames. Everyone felt her mood and responded to it. She was like a piece of steel newly magnetized. Jan Pierce had always been acknowledged to be the prettiest girl in town, and now she took her place as the most ravishing. Her wit, her gaiety never slackened. She was above herself, and yet, in the midst of the laughter and attention, she scarcely knew what she was saying, nor why all faces were turned towards her. For this one evening, everything she did succeeded and by personal prowess she led her team to victory, spelling words which in her right senses she would have failed in often enough.

Mr. Driscoll, who had been giving out the words, at the end made a flowery oration and crowned her Queen of the Dictionary with a wreath of laurel from a bush in the back yard. The party then broke up into groups sitting about at ease, the girls on chairs and the young men on the floor, while May and her younger sister, Alice, passed about gingerbeer and doughnuts and the last of the winter apples.

It was partly by chance and partly by a kind of wilfulness that Janet found herself in a group of young people sitting beside Alan, with Flo on his other side and Alexander Hunt to her left. Alex was a tall dark boy, with a rather brooding face, which could light up suddenly when he smiled. He came from one of the poorer farms towards the coast and stayed during the school year in Thomaston with a widowed aunt. He'd always been different from the other children. Janet could remember a scene from their fourth grade days when Alex had once started home after school with an armful of books so big that he could hardly hold them.

"Whatever are you taking so many books for, Alexander?" Miss Gay, the teacher, had asked rather crossly.

Alex turned and answered with sudden vehemence, "I want to learn all about everything!"

Miss Gay and the children had laughed, except Janet, who had walked over to him, head in the air, and taken half the books.

"I'll help you," she said.

He had looked at her without speaking, but from that day there'd always been an alliance between them. As he grew older, Alex learned not to talk about his interests. Only Janet knew that he kept a notebook filled with poetry, not at all the sweet and singing verses of the period, but rough and uneven, with here and there a line which struck across the imagination like light between clouds. When he showed it to her, she thought as she read the poems that some of them might be about her, but he never said so. All the school knew that he could tackle any problem in Euclid and could remember history dates. He still did queer things like going off by himself to watch the ship-building at Lovell's Yards, or he might reach down to take up a handful of earth and study it as it ran through his fingers, and he talked to the duds of the class as though they were as important as anyone else.

Because he was interested in so many more things than they were, the other young men called Alex crazy. But they all liked him. He never seemed to want close friends nor to go around with any of the girls, but he had a darting sense of humor of his own and a curious kindliness that made people turn to him.

Now, out of some corner of his memory, he **began to** ask conundrums.

> " 'Two toads totally tired
>   Tried to trot to Tedberry town.
> How many Ts in that?'

Have you got the answer, Flo?"

Flo, who was in a glowering mood, thought a minute and shook her head.

"I'll say it again, slowly, and you can count," and Alex repeated, " 'Two toads totally tired,' " while Flo ticked off Ts on her fingers.

"Twelve," she said at last, "I make it twelve."

"And you make it wrong."

"Thirteen," volunteered a young man.

"Fifteen," said another. "You count the last sentence."

"Two," said Janet, "There are only two Ts in 'that.' "

"Good for you, Jan. Now see if you can do this one. Imagine that you're in India and a maharaja has asked you to come to the palace and sends his elephant to fetch you. Would you know how to get down from an elephant?"

"No, only from a goose. I never saw anything stuffed with elephant's down."

"You've heard them before," exclaimed Flo crossly. "It's no fun playing when you know all the answers."

"I've never heard them before," said Janet. "I'm not so fond of cheating as some people I could name."

"And what do you mean by that?"

But before Janet could answer, Alex Hunt had interrupted.

"If you don't want to play conundrums, Flo, I'll read your future by apple seeds."

"I don't want any fortune telling."

"Read mine," said Alan, who hadn't spoken until then. He began to search the core of his apple for seeds.

"I must have eaten some. I can only find two."

"Alan always likes his things in pairs," said someone.

Alex ignored the talk.

"Two means marriage, Alan. I guess we'll see you step off any day now."

Janet felt her heart beating faster.

"Alex, wait, read mine!" She found one seed and then two. Oh, that was all she wanted to find, but the treacherous core split open and there was another seed and then another and then one more, and that was all.

" 'Two means marriage,
    Three means a legacy,
    Four means great wealth,
    Five means a long journey.' "

Flo looked at her and said disagreeably, "I'll be down at the station to wave you good-by."

"Wait until you hear I'm going."

"Oh, I'll wait."

"You'd better have your fortune read, Flo," Alex again interrupted, reaching out and taking Flo's core from the floor beside her and beginning to count the seeds, while the others watched.

Three seeds. ("Thank goodness she didn't have two. I couldn't have borne it," thought Janet.)

Four seeds and no more.

" 'Great Wealth,' " said Flo, preening. "I guess that's true anyhow."

"Well, I know I have six seeds even without looking," declared Alex, with an irony he kept for himself. " 'Six means great fame' and that's what I'm headed for."

Mr. Driscoll's jolly thick voice suddenly boomed out behind them, joined, voice by voice, by the others:

"Hi! says the blue jay as she flew,
  If I was a young man I'd have two;
  If one proved fickle and chanced to go,
  I'd have another string to my bow."

Well as Janet knew the "Birds' Courting Song," the words took on a new and bitter meaning for her now. Could it be that she felt jealous of Flo? She thrust the idea from her indignantly. The group around her began clapping hands and taking up the song, but even now she did not sing with them.

"Hi! says the little leather-winged bat,
  I will tell you the reason that,
  The reason that I fly by night,
  Is because I've lost my heart's delight."

Janet suddenly felt faint. Why should the words of an old nonsense song she'd sung a hundred times all at once have the power to pierce her through and through? She felt so tired. She must go home, whatever home meant.

Without waiting for the song to be finished, Janet rose, smiling and nodding good-by to those about her, although they seemed as vague as shadows to her. Among the shadows, she found Mr. Driscoll leading the singing with a kitchen spoon and Mrs. Driscoll out in the kitchen and May and Alice and made her adieux to them all. Alex had risen to join her but fell back as Alan took her arm, in spite of some protest from Flo. As they walked down the steps, both stopped for a moment, meeting the full force of the moonlight, the silence and the sweetness of lilac blossoms. There was a bush in full bloom by the walk, and Alan broke off a spray and gave it to Janet.

Then he kissed her. In silence, Janet threw herself into his arms with a desperation that she had never felt before. In his arms, for the first time since her father had said "Sit down, Janet," she was safe. Now nothing could harm her, nothing could make her afraid.

But when they were once more walking down the path, one scraped hand held in his, Alan began to ask questions.

"You never hurt yourself like that just falling, Jan. What happened to you?"

She leaned against his arm.

"I kept slipping as I came down the trumpet vine."

"Whatever in the world made you come down the trumpet vine?"

"Father had locked me in my room."

She had expected another question but Alan was silent for a space and the only sound was of their matched footfalls.

Then he said, "He doesn't want us to get married. I was afraid he wouldn't, but I thought you could persuade him. What did he say?"

But Janet could not bring herself to repeat the things that her father had said. To speak them, to hear Alan's answers would be to make him defend himself and his family and she would not humiliate him.

[31]

"Dear," she said at last, stopping and looking up into his shadowed face, "he said nothing but silly things. He's unreasonable. He won't change. He says that if we marry he'll disinherit me. He says we mustn't see each other. But nothing can stop us from seeing each other, nor from marrying."

Alan's arm was tight about her, but when she looked up at him in the moonlight he was looking straight ahead and his face seemed suddenly tired.

" 'Lazy as a hound dog or a Loring,' " he muttered. She had never heard him speak bitterly before. "Was that it, Jan?"

And when she wouldn't answer, he went on:

"There's nothing else against me. Just that fool saying someone made up fifty years ago and which has stuck to us like a burr. Ever since I was a little boy, people have said it every time I failed in anything. Your father says it now, and when I look for a job this fall people will be saying it to themselves while I'm talking to them. A fine chance I have to succeed with that hanging round my neck before I begin!"

Janet, wrung with pity, threw her arms about him and after a moment he clung to her.

"It isn't true! It isn't true! I believe in you, Alan, I trust you, I know that you can take care of me. Oh, Alan, let's get married tonight, right now! We could harness up your horse and drive over to Warren to the justice of the peace. It isn't very late. And look what a beautiful night it is, all moonlight and the smell of lilacs. We'd be so happy! And then no one could separate us."

Alan swung Janet off her feet and kissed her and put her down again.

"We'll show them! Come along, darling. We'll show them whether we care for their lies." And he started off, striding along so fast that Janet had almost to run to keep up with him. She was perfectly happy. Youth and lilacs and moonlight and perfect trust should have their way under the bright wide sky of that enchanted night, while middle age and caution and authority slept in their dark, enclosed rooms.

"Oh, Alan, I do so love you," she murmured, breathlessly.

But already he was slowing his pace.

"Where would we go afterwards? I haven't any money. Only about sixty-nine cents."

"It doesn't matter. I've got my grandmother's emerald ring. We could do something."

"And then what would we do?"

"You'd get a job and I'd keep house for you."

"But suppose I couldn't get a job?"

"But of course you could."

"Not everyone does and I've never tried."

Janet felt despair rising again in her heart and tried to get back to the carefree certainty of a few minutes ago.

"I'd keep house for you under an oak tree and we'd catch fish and gather strawberries."

"Jan, this is terribly serious."

"Seriously, couldn't we live with your family until you get a job?"

"I don't think Father and Mother would approve. You see it's pretty hard sledding for us as it is. Another person to take care of isn't anything that they'd welcome."

Janet still fought for their happiness.

"Oh, Alan, if we only *do* it, if we only *get* married, the rest will work out somehow. It always does. But first we have to show them that we love each other and that nothing can separate us!"

"Do you mean that you think your father would forgive you?"

There was a sudden eagerness in Alan's voice, which for all her desperation Janet recognized. He wanted to hitch up the black and drive off with her under the moon but he was afraid, afraid of the future. If she answered, "I think there's a good chance Father would," Alan still would go. But a resoluteness within herself made her certain of her father's resoluteness. For a moment she was tempted to give some half-truth, to sway Alan even now to what she felt with all her soul was the best thing for their love, but she couldn't build their happiness on half-truth.

"He might forgive us, but he'd never go back on what he said about his money."

"Well, then, we have to be sensible, Jan. We'll have to play for time. If I get a job your father may feel differently about me. He can't stand out against you and your mother."

"You don't know Father."

"You don't seem to know much about him, either." Janet had never heard Alan's tone with this icy sharpness in it. "You never once suggested that your father wouldn't approve of our engagement. You let me tell my family and all, and now I'm going to look like thirty cents."

"But I never once thought that anyone *could* object! It seemed so perfect. Alan, you don't mean that you think I didn't tell you on purpose?"

He softened at the horror in her tone.

"I was just teasing."

He tried to kiss her but she turned away her face. When

[34]

he put up his hands and forced her face towards him and kissed her on the mouth, she began to cry.

"But what *are* we to do, then?"

"Come along. We can't stand here. You've said your piece and now I'll say mine. How long will your father be here?"

"He usually is home for about a month."

"Then tomorrow I'll go to Uncle William's farm. He's short of hands and has been pestering me to come out to help him. I'll stay until after your father's gone. Then he won't get his dander up seeing me around the place. When he's gone, I'll come back and we'll see. Lots of things straighten out by themselves."

"But that's just running away."

"Sometimes running away's the best thing a person can do."

Janet didn't answer. Her feet felt heavy, like weights which she had to drag along, and that was hard because her body seemed dead. She didn't even want to cry.

Alan spoke out of the silence. "Now just do things my way for a change and you'll see that everything will work out."

"But will it work out right?"

"Of course," Alan said cheerfully.

For a moment, Janet was very close to rebellion. Part of her wanted to say that Alan was finding the easy way out, leaving her alone. But if that were true, what else might not be true? With a superb effort of heart and will she forced herself to trust him. Alan was a man and stronger and wiser than she was. He took a long view and could plan, and she would show him that she would follow his

[35]

plans without question as a woman should. She brought out her handkerchief and dried her eyes.

"Don't pay any attention to me. I'm tired. What will you do on the farm, Alan? Maybe I could come and be the dairymaid."

Alan smiled slightly and Janet raised the spray of lilac to her face and smelled it, feeling the little uneven flowers against her skin. Alan had broken it off for her to give her pleasure. They were nearing their own houses, dark in the moonlight. No, not quite dark. In the heart of the Pierce house, from some back room, perhaps Captain Pierce's study, a faint glow of light stole into the hall and through the frosted glass of the front door. It was a mere tarnish of yellow in that world of white moonlight and blue-black shadow, but it was menacing none the less.

"I'll say good night now," said Alan at the gate. "It's much better that I shouldn't meet your father. You can tell him you came home alone."

"I can't lie," thought Janet. Yet she clung to Alan and returned his kisses with all her heart. "You'll write me often? I shall miss you every minute of the day and night."

"Not too often. We've got to be careful. And I'll enclose my notes to you in letters to Mother. Remember the thing to do is to win over your father. Don't go against him."

"But I have to go against him if I'm to love you and to love you is the breath of my life." This she said to him not in words, but in their parting kisses, the lilac crushed and fragrant between them. Alan turned away at last.

"Better get it over."

But as she started up the front walk, he changed his mind and overtook her to take her in his arms once more. There was something different in the way he held her and kissed her, and the way he said, "I shall never love anyone else in all my life as I love you now."

Bewildered, shaken by the tenderness of his tone, Janet turned again towards the house. There was one more thing to be endured that night before she could hope for rest. Already Alan had vanished like a shadow, perhaps a watchful shadow. But her only help lay in her own soul. Without trying the door to see if by any chance it were unlocked so that she might creep in unnoticed, she pulled at the knob of the doorbell and rang it boldly.

CHAPTER IV

The Apple Seeds Were Right

THE bell pealed through the house as the last trump might sound in a tomb, and then the slow unhurried tread of Captain Pierce was heard coming down the hall and the door opened. Before speaking, the Captain lighted the gas jet by the stairs and, turning, said, as though to an acquaintance, "Did you have a pleasant evening, Janet? You're home earlier than I had expected."

Whatever Janet had braced herself for, it was not this, but she met it warily.

"Very pleasant, Father, thank you. Has Mother gone to bed?"

"Yes. I am finishing a letter to your Aunt Ione, but shall be up shortly."

"Good night, Father."

"Good night, Janet."

He even added "Sleep well," as she mounted the stairs, but whether in irony or kindness she had no idea.

There was no sound from her mother's room as she tiptoed by. Perhaps Mrs. Pierce had really gone to sleep, tired out by the emotions of the day. The hall presented a row of blank closed doors. When she opened her own, her room reproved her by its moonlit serenity. How many,

many nights she had slept in her bed and dreamed only happy dreams! But tonight she was too tired even to undress and too unhappy to care, and pulling off her slippers she threw herself as she was on the quilt and so fell asleep with her face turned towards the windows and towards Alan. All night her dreams were troubled and filled with vague shapes and runaway horses and lilac branches, which broke in her hands as she clung to them to save herself. Sometimes, she recognized her father among the shapes, but she never saw Alan, although it was for him that she was searching by land and sea, in one of those nightmares where the dreamer can never find what he must endlessly try to find among all the changing forms of his dreams.

When Janet woke, a robin was singing loudly from the lilac bush below her windows and a soft spring rain was falling, drip, drip, drip, beading with clear transparent drops the branches and sliding slowly from one cluster of wet and heavy leaves to another, and then to another, and at last to the velvet morass of the lawn. It must have been raining for some time. Where were the moon and the bright enchanted night? They had been too perfect to endure and Janet was grateful to this slow sodden rain, so monotonous, so gentle and so sad. As she lay listlessly watching, she heard a door slam—probably behind Stephen—and then fell asleep once more and roused again only when the clock at the foot of the stairs struck one, two, three, four, five, six, seven, eight, nine, ten in its deep resonant tones rather like her father's voice. Ten o'clock and no one had wakened her! In the Pierce household everyone got up at seven. Perhaps she was to be treated as a guest, not as a member of the family. A guest. How queer.

Ten o'clock! She raised herself on her elbow, looking to-

[39]

wards the Loring house. Was Alan still there? Should she see him? Surely she would once more watch him come through the back door slamming it behind him, whistling, unless he were eating one of his mother's cookies. Whistling, eating, blowing a kiss to her in the window! Was she never to see him in that carefree way again?

She heard hoofs and wheels scrunching and splashing on the uneven gravel of the Loring drive. She would know the black's hoof-beats anywhere, and at that sound the last fog of dreams left her and she jumped up and ran to kneel down by the window to look out. She saw the democrat, splashed with mud, disappearing into the stable, and after a while Mr. Loring's bulky figure came out, bundled up and dripping. There was no sign of Alan and what weighed upon Janet's heart was the basket which Mr. Loring carried in one hand. It was filled with eggs, across which lay a headless chicken still in its feathers.

He had certainly been at Mr. William Loring's farm and as certainly the only errand which could have sent him there early on a rainy morning would have been to take Alan away from her. Now the sun was doubly hidden for Janet; the light by which she really lived was taken from her.

Quietly she changed her clothes for fresh ones. Listlessly she came down the stairs. Her father had gone out on business, her mother was teaching Debby her spelling lesson, and the boys were at school. Norah brought in her breakfast to the dining room table. Minnie had been keeping the cereal hot on the back of the kitchen range but the tea was fresh. No one came in to speak to her, nothing moved but two flies at a window endlessly climbing up the pane and then

[40]

slipping down, only to climb again. Janet grew tired of watching them.

When Captain Pierce came home he acted as though nothing had happened, except that his household seemed to be made up of his wife, his son and two small children, and servants and a young woman guest. Janet, for her part, behaved like a sleepwalker. Her mother's uncertain, quick gestures of affection, Stephen's gruff rallying, the wide-eyed interest of Ted and little Debby could not awaken her from her daze. She went about quietly, answering when she was spoken to, smiling politely, trying to talk with her father about his last voyage. She remembered that Alan had told her that she must not antagonize her father, whatever she did.

The Captain, too, made an effort, but soon broke out, "You're not listening."

"Yes, I am, Father."

"You don't know a word I was saying. You'd better help your mother."

"But Mother doesn't need any help."

It was true that there was nothing pressing which called for Janet's attention. Work might have helped her, but there was no work to be done. Stephen, as time went on, grew uneasy at her languid politeness and said things which in former days would have led to a battle royal, but Janet scarcely heard him either, and Stephen retired to consult with his friend Millard.

Only when later in the week Janet went to Mrs. Loring's back door to ask if any news had come from Alan, did she become for a few minutes the old eager Janet, but as day followed day without a letter she grew ashamed to go

[41]

on asking. At last, one morning, Mrs. Loring tapped on the window as the girl went by, and when she hurried in there was a letter for her, a somewhat casual letter, filled with farm affairs but ending in a dozen crosses for kisses and circles for hugs. By this time, the lilacs were out of bloom and the blossoms were hardening to dead husks among the leaves. Even the birds were too busy feeding their young to sing much any more. Springtime was over and workaday, everyday summer had taken its place.

On the same day that Janet had her letter from Alan, Captain Pierce received an answer to his letter to his sister in Bristol. It came in the morning mail and he read it through without comment, but at luncheon he made his announcement:

"I heard from Sister Ione this morning and she says that she will be able to arrange her affairs so as to come with us. That will be much pleasanter for you, Janet. You will have another woman to talk to when I am necessarily busy."

Janet looked at her father in frank amazement, but she spoke gently.

"What do you mean, Father?"

"That you are going with me on my next voyage. We leave early in July and shall be gone a year and perhaps a little more, but it is to be a relatively short voyage."

Janet froze.

"You may be going, Father, but I am not."

"May I remind you that you are speaking to your father?"

"But that doesn't give you the right to carry me away from home against my will!"

"I beg to differ from you. It gives me exactly that right.

[42]

And I wish to hear nothing further from you on the subject. I expect you to be ready by the first of July."

The Captain turned to Mrs. Pierce, who sat with her hands twisting at her napkin, her eyes brimming with tears. For her, too, the announcement came without warning.

"Please help Janet with her wardrobe, Adelaide. You will remember from our wedding trip what she is likely to need on the voyage and along the China coast."

"Gosh! Don't waste it on Janet, Father," said Stephen. Debby, too, spoke up:

"If Janet doesn't want to go, I'll go, Father."

Captain Pierce smiled. "You'll have to wait your turn, Debby. Janet's a big girl now and she should go first and tell you about it so you'll know what to do when it's your turn."

"I can tell you now, Debby," cried Janet. "Run away from home the first chance you get and never let Father break your heart as he is breaking mine!"

"My! My!" mocked Stephen in a low voice, going on with his meal.

The younger children stared at Janet openmouthed, and the tears brimmed over Mrs. Pierce's eyes and fell unheeded to her dress. Only Captain Pierce was entirely unmoved.

"Will you ring, Adelaide, to have the table cleared?"

"Before Norah comes in, Father, I want to give you fair warning that I shall do everything in my power to keep you from doing this wicked thing."

"Certainly, Janet. I expect no less. And I have taken my own measures so far as I could foresee your probable behavior. I respect your honesty and hold no ill will, though surely I have a right to expect from you an obedience

[43]

which I am not being accorded. Should you wish to be excused now to go to your own chamber, you have your mother's and my permission."

"You speak for us all, don't you, Father?" Janet smiled, but it was a smile very new to her lips. "I prefer to stay for dessert and coffee."

That very afternoon Mrs. Pierce began to go over Janet's clothes, making lists of everything which would be needed for the next twelve or fourteen months in a variety of climates. The task brought with it its own contentment, reminding her vividly of her trip to the Orient as a bride and of the strange ports she had visited and the sights and sounds which she had almost forgotten. Several times, she tried to tell Janet something of what lay ahead, but the girl would not listen. The third time she came over to where her mother was standing, counting neat piles of petticoats and camisoles, and kissed her.

"Mother dear," she said, "you'd like to help me if you could, and I know that. But you can't win me over to wanting to go on the *Phoenix*. Obey Father if you must, but don't talk about the trip. I can't stand it, I really can't stand it! There's no one to help me and I don't know what to do."

And with the words echoing in her ears, she set out to do something, hurrying down the stairs and out of the house and running next door to see Mrs. Loring.

Mrs. Loring was a fat worried-looking woman, still handsome in a way, but it was not from her that Alan had taken his singular beauty.

She greeted Janet kindly and took her into the parlor, seating her on the haircloth sofa and sitting beside her, her large work-rough hand still holding Janet's fine fingers.

"Now don't say a word, dear. I can guess what you've

come for. The Captain wrote me a letter a few days ago. I'd like to invite you to stay here but a quarrel between the families would prejudice people against Alan next fall when he tries to make a start. You wouldn't want to do that, would you? You know the Captain is very much respected in the town. It's not safe to go against him. Life is sad," she went on, squeezing Janet's fingers. "I've found it sad. We can't always have what we set our hearts on in this world, Janet dear."

Janet rose, breathing hurriedly to hold back the tears.

"Thank you, Mrs. Loring," she said, and went slowly home and upstairs to her room.

Next she wrote to Alan, a desperate cry for help, begging him to take her away. A letter from him crossed with hers. It was very loving and written more seriously than any word she had ever had from him. He had heard of the projected plan from her father.

"There is nothing we can do now," he wrote her, and went on to advise her to go with her father and to enjoy herself. He would get work and would throw himself into it with so much good will that he would surely have been promoted by the time she and her father returned. Then her father would be forced to reconsider. The end of the letter moved her more than anything he had ever said to her.

"Surely you trust me to be true to you, and I know your brave heart and would trust to your love if you were going to be away ten years instead of one."

Although Alan had made no offer to return or to take her away, Janet was much comforted. Suddenly neither time nor space frightened her any more. With an exultant relief she thought, "What's a year? Or China? Alan and I *love* each other." Could it be that she had not quite trusted him? Was that why she had been in such despair? How unworthy of her! How unworthy of their love! Never, never, never again would she belittle the beautiful thing they shared by displaying such meanness of spirit.

Miss Nellie Brewster, the sewing woman, came to stay at the house and began cutting out woolen frocks, and cotton frocks with ruffles, and heavy cloaks and light cloaks, and Janet endured the necessary fittings in silence, but took no part in the discussions between her mother and the dressmaker, nor would she look into the mirror to see her reflection there.

She continued still in her efforts to find some place which would shelter her. She wrote to her favorite aunt and uncle, who lived in Portland, to ask if she might come to them on a long visit and was scarcely surprised to receive in return a gentle refusal. She wrote to the school board asking for a position as teacher and was told that there were no vacancies left. Everywhere she saw that her father had been before her, locking the door which she sought to open.

Meanwhile, the days followed one another, and instead of lilacs, the first hay carts filled the street with their passing fragrance. Janet's boxes were almost packed; her shoes had been made by the village shoemaker; and one day there was a ring at the door, and when Norah opened it, she found Susan Mann, Betsey Prince Trask and three or four other girls, asking to see Janet. Norah ushered them into the parlor and when Janet hurried in, they all surrounded her with a host of questions and endearments. They had brought her a friendship handkerchief with their names in their various handwritings embroidered about the hem. Flo was there with the other girls and her name, too, was

[46]

on the handkerchief. She took the first possible opportunity to remark, "You see, the apple seeds were right, Janet! You're going on a journey, after all." And rattled on, "Poor Father isn't feeling a bit well."

"So you'll get a fortune, Flo?" Janet asked.

She looked at Flo's heavy aggressive face with horror. She was angry with her own father, but she had never once thought of his death as a way out of her difficulties. Yet Flo talked of the possibility of her indulgent father's dying as matter-of-factly as she'd talk of buying a new bonnet. At Janet's question now, Flo shrugged her shoulders, smiling, and answered, "Maybe."

But little Annie Pratt, perched on the piano stool, spoke right up for them all.

"You ought to be ashamed to talk like that, Flo! What's money compared to someone you love?"

"Money's a pretty nice thing to have," Flo answered, quite unabashed. "And sometimes having it or not having it makes a lot of difference with someone you love, don't it, Janet?"

Janet made no answer. She could not deal with Flo's vulgarity. But neither was she troubled by it. Her love and trust were now absolute and Flo disturbed her neither more nor less than a toad might, sunning itself on the step and darting out its ugly tongue for flies, though she was glad when the girls trouped out again into the sunlight and left her to her thoughts.

Her father and Janet were to take the train to Boston on Tuesday, meeting Aunt Ione at the Parker House, and sailing in two days. Mrs. Pierce could not come with them as she didn't like to leave Stephen and the children.

Janet had no way of knowing that Steve and his best

friend, Millard, a skinny energetic boy with big hands, had become her champions since her rebellion. Something about her manner had touched their pity and respect, and from that moment they were ready to serve her, often talking her situation over as they loitered in Millard's front yard. They had magnificent plans, including the kidnapping of Captain Pierce, but nothing as yet had been achieved. Janet didn't even know of their new devotion, which they were so careful to hide that, in actual fact, they seemed, if anything, more annoying than usual when she was around.

Late Monday afternoon after the heat of the sun had left the garden, Janet went out to cut some flowers for the house. The peonies were at their height, and many of them smelled like roses. Her mother was busy, her father had gone off on business, Stephen, as usual, was away from home, Teddy and Debby, too, were off on their own affairs. Janet was glad to be alone, cutting the great heads one by one and laying them in the flat flower basket. She had no idea that anyone else had come into the garden, until a hand closed over her eyes and a well-known arm went about her waist.

CHAPTER V

Boston

ALL her life Janet would remember the sweetness of that stolen half hour, so unexpected and so swiftly gone. Alan and she were alone again; at least, if there were anyone else left in the world Janet didn't know it. Alan's arms were around her, his kisses were on her cheeks, her lips. Then at last he held her off so that they might look at one another.

An expression of surprise crossed his handsome face.

"You don't look sick, Jan!" he exclaimed. "Why did you say you were sick?" His voice held a faint note of irritation.

She looked back, bewildered.

"I never said I was sick!" she replied. "Honestly, Alan, I don't know what you're talking about."

"You didn't tell Steve and Millard to write me that you were dying?"

The look of astonishment on her face convinced him, and suddenly he began to laugh.

"I might have known that there was nothing in it, but I fell for it. Wait till I lay my hands on them! But never mind. I'm here now and it gives us a chance to say good-by. As long as your father doesn't find out, it doesn't matter."

And as though there had been no interruption, he went on with his love-making.

For a moment Janet was furious with the boys, but only for a moment. They had brought her this happiness. She would be grateful to them until her dying day.

After a little they began to talk, mostly about Alan and what he had been doing or would do. It was all wonderful to Janet, but before they had said half enough, Steve appeared around the corner of the Loring house calling raucously: "Kitty! Kitty! Kitty! Come, Kitty! Come, Kitty!"

Alan kissed Janet again hastily.

"Good-by, darling! I must run. The boys have been watching for your father and that's the signal that he's coming!" And with a laugh, he kissed her once more, gave her a hug, and was off down the garden path, across the lawn, had vaulted the picket fence, and with a final sprint across the Lorings' rather ragged grass, vanished through the back door with a last wave of the hand, just as Captain Pierce appeared along the sidewalk. Janet's impulse was to tell her father that she had seen Alan, but she kept silent and went on cutting flowers, since that was what Alan seemed to prefer. Alan was wiser than she, and she would do everything his way, not hers. She did get hold of Steve that evening and thanked him.

"It isn't right to tell lies and to mix up in other people's business, but, oh, I can't help but be glad you did!" She said, and Steve turned red and answered evasively. But suddenly she felt that he loved her, and in surprise and gratitude, she leaned over and kissed his cheek.

"Hi! Look out what you're doing!" he protested, but he was delighted. If only he could manage to kidnap the Captain or something!

The next day Janet took the train for Boston with her father, and all her friends came to see her off, including Flo Andrews, looking like an ill-favored cat snug in the softest chair. There was no sign of Alan, though until the very last moment Janet's eyes searched for him behind the others and at the windows of the station. She could not believe that he would not be there. Alex Hunt seemed to understand her quick glances and said in an undertone as he shook hands with her: "He didn't want a row with your father. It will be all right. I'll do everything I can to help you." And then he added in a low voice that she scarcely heard, "You know I'd do anything for you."

For a moment, just a moment, memories rushed into her mind of the number of times Alex had been there when she needed him. "But not me, especially," she thought, "he's that way with everyone." She pressed his hand gratefully.

"Thank you, Alex. Give Alan my love."

His face looked graver than she had ever seen it.

"Yes," he said, and then, "We'll all miss you, Jan."

The others pressed in, girls and boys with whom she had grown up, they were saying good-by, shaking her hand and the girls were kissing and hugging her.

Susan Mann was crying.

"I think it's a shame!" said outspoken Annie Pratt, standing on tiptoe to kiss Janet. "You're being just dragged off. We're all going to miss you. Your father is mean!"

Such a hubbub surrounded her that she could scarcely tell one voice from another, one face from the next.

"Good-by, good-by! Thank you all for coming! Good-by!"

There was a thunder and clanging along the track and the thick puffing of an engine.

"Train's in!" called Captain Pierce, who was standing a little apart with his wife and Steve and the children. "Come, Janet."

Her mother in tears embraced her. "Oh, my darling! Do try to be happy."

Steve kissed her awkwardly.

"Don't get lost," he tried to joke, and then added in an undertone, "Millard and me will keep an eye on things here."

Debby and Ted were more conscious of the excitement than of its cause. They had brought their Fourth-of-July flags and, shouting shrilly, waved them in everyone's face.

Janet, between laughter and tears, was helped up the steps by her father, followed by a veritable barricade of luggage. The engine whistled, the conductor cried "All aboard!" and with a jerk and a snort the little train was off. Even as Janet waved good-by to her mother and the others, she still looked for Alan, and as the people on the station platform dwindled, she lingered where she was, watching eagerly along the well-known roads and fields of Thomaston, hoping to see his figure standing somewhere waving good-by.

Captain Pierce did not hurry her, but as the houses blurred and shifted position in the distance, he put her hand in his arm, and led her into the car.

"It's better so, Janet," he remarked quietly. "Put all that in the past and leave it behind you."

She turned on him hotly, her eyes wide and dry.

"Do you put Mother and the children behind you?"

"That's a different matter."

"The only difference is that I love Alan more than anyone ever loved anybody in the world. If he didn't come to see me off, he had a good reason for it and it doesn't make me unhappy a bit," and with that she started to cry and had to find her handkerchief. But soon she dried her eyes with an effort. It was the first time that her father had seen her in tears since a morning when she was ten years old and discovered that the family cat had climbed up the apple tree and taken all the baby robins from the nest that she had been watching. He was glad now when she regained her self-mastery, though he knew that the tears were still there unshed behind her gray-green eyes, as they sped on and on towards Boston and the unknown.

Janet had only once been in Boston and that was some years ago when she was still a child, as she now considered, though at thirteen she had seemed to herself very much a young lady in her plaid coat, with a long braid down her back. She remembered the view up the Mall to the golden dome of the State House and the pigeons in the Gardens by a pond and the rolls which they had had for dinner and for which the hotel was famous—although they seemed no better to her than Minnie's. But as they drove to the hotel from the North Station, a great many forgotten memories were refreshed in her mind, like dry shells and pebbles on a beach when a wave washes over them and brings out all the colors.

She remembered the smell of ground coffee, and the masts of vessels by the wharves, and the unaccustomed noise of crowds, and the smart look of the women going in and out of the great stores. It was a warm day, but not hot as yet, though the thunderheads were beginning to pile up above the buildings.

Suddenly her father broke the silence between them by saying, "See, the gulls."

Looking up, she saw a dozen of the white creatures floating over the city.

"Your aunt will be waiting for us," he went on. "You two will probably wish to do some shopping this afternoon. She will be able to advise you, being older and more experienced."

"I don't want to go shopping," Janet began.

"Nonsense!" her father interrupted. "I wish you to go, and that's an end to it."

Janet suddenly had a thought. "Certainly, Father," she said.

But he seemed to know what was going on in her mind.

"Your aunt will carry the money. You might mislay it, and although I don't mind having money used, I should not wish to have it wasted."

The hope, which had never been clearly formulated, died. Janet turned her attention to a squabble between some newsboys. As the cab drew up at the hotel, two colored porters came out to take their luggage. They both seemed to know Captain Pierce.

"How are you, Captain?" one of them said. "Glad to see you back, sir." The other, an older man, with a lean black face and cloudy eyes gave her a look of recognition. She saw that his feet hurt him and he hobbled as he walked. The veins on the hands holding the luggage stood far out from the flesh. He was an old man, and she was ashamed not to remember him when he remembered her, but she felt oddly touched by his knowing her.

Aunt Ione was not at the hotel after all, and Janet was glad to be, for a little while, alone in her room, which opened out from her aunt's by a connecting door. A maid came in with hot water and fresh towels, and she washed at the heavy walnut stand. The mirror, very bright and new, gave back her image. She looked at her face, at her hair combed high, with curls at the back, at her long eyebrows, and her gray-green eyes, and her mouth, looking quite red against her white skin. She was amazed that her face seemed to show nothing of the misery of her heart. She wondered about other people, the people on the train and on the streets. Behind their commonplace expressions and gestures, did some of them feel despairs and joys quite hidden away from sight? Of course, she thought, older people couldn't feel the way she felt. They had worn off the edges of emotion long ago. But the young people? Were they all living in secret behind their faces, and no one guessing?

Her room faced into other buildings and over roofs. It had a dark red paper on the walls and at the windows there were heavy red curtains which smelled of cigar smoke. The furniture was of walnut except for the big brass bed, looking smart and citified. On one wall hung two framed pictures of a young man and a young lady in eighteenth century costumes. One was called "Good Morning" and the other was "Good Night" and there wasn't much difference, except that the lady was coming down the stairs in one and going up them in the other, and the lady and young man both looked happy to be seeing each other in the morning and sad at parting in the evening. The frames were very fancy, and the pictures were sentimental and unreal, but they were intended to portray love, and Janet's eyes filled with tears as she looked at them.

There was a tap at her door and when she opened it she found her father and Aunt Ione, a small woman with an unnoticeable face, lightened by two eyes of an almost disconcerting blue. She kissed Janet warmly, but as Janet was reserved, she turned back to the Captain.

"Have them put my things in my room, if you please, John. Later on, Janet and I will go out to see Boston. What time is dinner? Very well, we'll be ready at six."

During the afternoon Aunt Ione behaved like any agreeable stranger. She asked Janet no questions and made no personal remarks, nor did she talk about her own affairs. Janet knew that she was a widow and lived in her husband's house at Bristol, Rhode Island. Richard Pattison had been a missionary in Korea and Aunt Ione had met him at Shanghai when she was a girl taking a voyage with her own father. They had been married two weeks after their first meeting and she had lived in the Orient for ten years without ever coming to America. Two years ago they had returned to Bristol when Uncle Richard was fatally ill, and he had died there. Janet had never seen either of them.

"I suppose she's only thirty-three or four," Janet thought once, but Aunt Ione was really so homely and so competent that she didn't seem at all young, or as though she had ever been young. She guided Janet in and out of stores, and something in her bright blue glance gained them instant service wherever they appeared. She said little to Janet, yet the girl felt her judgment guided and confirmed in the purchases she made. Janet scarcely cared enough to make any decisions, but Aunt Ione had a short list which Janet's mother had made out, and they went methodically down it, and at every purchase Aunt Ione crossed out an item with a small gold pencil, which she took out of her handbag.

When the last thing, a pair of high-buttoned shoes, had

been bought and was being wrapped up, Janet rose with a sigh and looked about her. The store was empty except for a few clerks and a mother with two small children who had just come in. Through the show windows she could see the crowd like a flowing river, with each human drop bent on some errand of its own. A longing came over her to mix with it and be lost, but she looked down at the handbag in her hand. There were about thirty-six cents in it. With the ghost of a smile, she took the package from the clerk and followed Aunt Ione out of the store.

A church bell rang five o'clock overhead and Aunt Ione said, "We had better go back to the hotel and rest a little while before dinner. Shall we walk or would you like to take a cab?"

But Janet preferred to walk, to prolong the moment under the open sky before the hotel closed about her again like a prison. It was not darker, but the lowered sun was less hot and a touch of twilight breeze moved through the streets. In her vague mood, she found herself almost stumbling over a legless man, seated on a piece of carpet with his back against a building, selling pencils, his crutches beside him, while his greasy cap, with a scattering of small coins in it, lay upside down on the pavement, mutely appealing.

Janet started back, her eyes widening. She had never seen a cripple before, except for Rufe Hardigan, who had lost his right arm at the sawmill, and he was different, running his own farm like anyone else, with help from his wife and his daughter, Polly.

"Wait, Aunt Ione," she said. She took the thirty-six cents out of her bag and placed them carefully in the old cap, her head nearly on a level with the man's. "I wish I had more," she apologized.

[57]

"Thank you, miss." She was surprised that his face, too, looked almost like anyone's else.

"Here!" he called after her. "You forgot to take your pencil."

"Take it," said Aunt Ione in a low voice, and Janet went back and took the red pencil which he held out to her with a smile. There was almost a fleeting pity in his glance as though the man were thinking, "Where have you been that you didn't know the world was full of people like me and worse? You'll learn quick enough."

As she rejoined her aunt, Janet had an impulse to throw away the red pencil. She didn't want to see it and to have to think about the legless man each time. But she put it instead into her pocket-book, empty of money now.

She and Alan would be all right. They loved each other. Love laughs at locksmiths. In a year or two, she'd be back and Alan would be earning money and they'd get married. But the man with the pencils—in a year or two he'd be just the same as he was now.

CHAPTER VI

The Sisters

"I HAVE good news for you, Janet," said the Captain that night, as the three sat together at a small table in the crowded dining room. A pianist and violinist were playing a waltz, and the Negro waiters moved among tables crowded with men in evening clothes and ladies in gowns such as Janet had never seen. To the girl's surprise, Aunt Ione seemed quite at home in these surroundings. Homely as ever, she yet looked smart and fashionable, glancing about her calmly, and now and then nodding and smiling to some acquaintance at another table.

Janet, in her homemade dress, felt awkward and shy and held her head the higher. What did it all matter anyway? she thought, and never realized that she was the most beautiful woman in the room. She did not even realize how much she was being looked at. Only the admiration in one pair of eyes meant anything to her, and they were far away.

"What is the good news, John?" Aunt Ione asked, for Janet had not heard what her father said.

"Lydia is coming tomorrow and will stay overnight and see us off."

Janet's attention was caught by her sister's name.

"Is Jo coming?" she inquired, but the Captain shook his head.

"He is away on business."

Lydia arrived the next morning a little before eleven. Janet and Aunt Ione were in the lobby waiting for her, but they did not at first recognize her in her very up-to-date dress with its bustle and leg-of-mutton sleeves, especially as she was wearing over her flowered hat a green veil, which almost hid her face. They were both astonished when an apparent stranger ran up to them and threw her arms about them.

Janet hadn't seen her sister for two years and she was surprised by the change in her. She seemed much older and she talked and laughed a great deal more than Janet remembered. She was very gay and affectionate with them both, for she had visited Aunt Ione and was apparently fond of her, and when she wasn't talking about Jo and their little house she was reminiscing about Thomaston.

"Oh, do you remember the time we tried to ride the Lorings' colt, Jan?" she would ask. "You stuck on longest, but we both came home covered with mud. Mother told us it wasn't ladylike. And how is Miss Griffith who taught English and French? And is my rosebush doing well? I wish you'd brought some dried alewives with you! I haven't tasted one since I left home."

Janet listened and answered when she could, for Lydia darted from subject to subject and scarcely waited for an answer from anyone. When the Captain arrived for luncheon, she seemed gayer than ever, and, as he listened to her, his face relaxed from the rather stern expression, which it had worn lately.

"So you still think well of Jo?" he asked affectionately.

Lydia laughed and her pretty face flushed with happiness.

"Jo's the most wonderful man in the world and I'm the luckiest girl," she answered. "He did so want to come to see you all, but his time isn't his own, alas! He's so valuable to his company that they're always sending him off nowadays to represent them in other cities. I might almost as well have been like Mamma and married a sailor."

She laughed again and Aunt Ione patted her hand.

"There, dear, eat your lunch. You've scarcely touched anything yet and you'll be hungry."

"Oh, I'm never hungry, Aunt Ione. I'm too excited to eat."

"Try anyhow. Everyone needs to eat."

Janet, like her father, was more herself with Lydia there to rattle on. She and Lydia had had a very pleasant sisterly relationship when they lived under one roof, though with four years' difference in their ages, they seldom did much together. Lydia as a girl had been pretty, dark-eyed and dark-haired, gentle and obedient. This vivacity was something rather new. "But marriage changes people," Janet thought. "She's so happy it bubbles out of her; perhaps I'll be like this when Alan and I are married." And for a fleeting moment, she remembered that once she had been rather like this but for different reasons. She had been unhappy at the spelling bee, not happy like Lydia. But, perhaps, any emotion may be enough to make a girl's cheeks rosy and her eyes bright.

After lunch, the Captain had once more to go to the owner's office, and Aunt Ione said that she had a letter or two to write and that she would stay in the lobby; she suggested that the girls might like to rest and talk.

[61]

"You must have a great deal to tell one another," she said, rather sadly.

"I've been talking a blue streak all morning, Auntie," Lydia laughed, and Aunt Ione smiled affectionately without answering except for saying, "Off with you, now! I shan't be up for another hour."

As the door of Janet's bedroom closed behind them, Janet flung herself into Lydia's arms.

"Oh, Lydia," she sobbed, "you won't be able to understand. You've got Jo and everything you want in the world. But I'm so unhappy that sometimes I hope I'll die. They won't let me marry Alan."

Lydia patted her shoulder and clung to her, half laughing, half crying.

"Oh, won't I understand!" she gulped. "I'm unhappier than you are. Alan wants you, doesn't he? I knew it. But Jo hates the sight of me. That's why he wouldn't come today. He makes any excuse to get away."

Janet could scarcely believe her ears.

"Lydia!" she cried, "Why, Jo adores you. You're crazy."

Lydia went over to the washstand and, wetting the end of a towel, wiped her eyes, patted her hair—looking in the mirror—and turned to face Janet. She was quiet now and her face was set.

"Jan, you're lucky to be going away. I wish I were in your shoes. Don't get married if you're in love; it's torture day and night. As soon as a man's married, he stops being in love. I wish Jo and I had never laid eyes on each other."

Janet was horrified.

"You mean you don't love him any more?"

Lydia shrugged.

"Yes, I still love him. That's the trouble."

"But he wrote such wonderful letters to us."

"The first two or three months. Then he began to change. I tried not to see it at first and was just more loving and gay than ever. But it gets worse and worse. My heart is breaking; all I pray for now is to die or to stop loving him."

Janet put her arms about Lydia again but Lydia only patted her cheek in a grown-up fashion.

"Just count your blessings, dear," she advised solemnly as Janet stood back. "Being in love is wonderful when someone's in love with you. You have that—and a voyage to China and Japan—that's wonderful. Why should you be unhappy? You're so beautiful, Jan. I'd almost forgotten. You have everything. If you stop being in love with Alan, all the better; then you can marry him and you won't care."

Janet covered her face with her hands.

"Lydia!" she cried sharply. "Don't talk like that! It's like a dead person talking."

Lydia smiled.

"I feel like a dead person."

Janet looked at her again. "But you seemed so happy this morning—and at lunch—"

"That's the way I am all the time now. Everyone thinks I'm happy—even Jo; but Aunt Ione knew."

"I'm so sorry."

"You needn't be sorry. Perhaps all women feel like this after they're married."

"Mother doesn't!"

"How do we know? You didn't even guess how I felt and I'm still young. I'm not quite twenty-two and I'll lie like this all my life."

"Lydia, Lydia, stop! It's terrible to hear you talk like

this. I love Alan and Alan loves me, and we'd never be like Jo and you, never! Never! Never!"

"Never is a long time," said Lydia. "First you begin to realize that he isn't listening, and then that he's trying to avoid you, and at last that he'd rather be anywhere than in the same room with you. When we go out together now, he leaves me as soon as he decently can and talks and laughs with anyone at all. If I join the group he's with, he becomes silent, though he may have been laughing the minute before. I get perfectly desperate. I don't know what I'm saying half the time. It's awful to feel that Jo despises me."

Janet, trying to reassure Lydia, was also trying to reassure herself.

"Darling, Jo *must* feel the same underneath. Why, he used to think the sun rose and set for you. If you could only go away for a little while—"

Lydia took it up eagerly.

"If I only could! Here I'd give anything to be sailing with Father, and you'd give anything to be staying home and seeing Alan! Oh yes, I know all about what's happened. Steve's written me to ask me to help you. Its perfectly clear that you two think that you're in love and that Father doesn't approve. I wish he had felt the same when Jo and I wanted to get married!"

Janet was scarcely listening. She had sunk down into a chair and was sitting, hands clasped in her lap, her eyes wide open, a small breathless smile on her face.

All at once she jumped up and caught Lydia by the shoulders.

"Lydia!" she exclaimed, staring into her sister's face, "Lydia, would you dare do it?"

"Dare?" asked Lydia, staring back. "What do you mean, dare?"

Janet began to laugh excitedly.

"Why shouldn't we change places? You go on the *Phoenix* and I go home? We could do it. People in books do it all the time. We're almost the same height. If I wore your dress and that green veil and pretended to be in a hurry and crying, no one would know me."

"And where would I be?"

"You'd be in the cabin with the door locked and crying so hard you wouldn't let anyone in. Father would never know until you were out to sea."

"And too late to go back! And you'd write Jo!"

"And then when he'd lost you, he'd know that he loved you and he'd be sorry that he'd made you so unhappy."

"I wonder if he would? But, Jan, I wouldn't dare. Father would be furious."

"Father has been furious with me for days and that's the least of my worries. After a while, he'd forgive you and you'd have a wonderful time together. You'd forget all your troubles and when you came home, Jo'd be waiting as the *Phoenix* sailed down the harbor."

"And you and Alan would be safely married, even if you had to run away. Jan, it's too wonderful to work out that way. There'd be some catch in it. Maybe Jo'd be glad I'd gone, and Alan might still be afraid to marry you."

"Lydia, we'd be no worse off than we both are now, and we would have a chance anyhow. If we aren't willing to risk anything for our happiness, we don't deserve it. What are you afraid of? You say you have nothing to lose and yet you say that you're afraid."

[65]

Janet's face was lighted with sudden hope. Resourceful, fearless, she swept away Lydia's protests. The whole plan seemed to work out smoothly. At the last moment, in the *Phoenix* stateroom, they would put on one another's clothes. Then, when the vessel was about to sail, Janet in Lydia's dress and veil would hurry out, say a muffled good-by and go ashore! Lydia would remain hidden and trust to sobs to disguise her voice until they were out to sea. Then let the Captain storm! He could get on with the daughter who wanted to go.

"But suppose he suspects?" Lydia asked in final doubt.

"Why should he? He thinks you're as happy as the day is long."

"Aunt Ione might."

Janet considered this.

"You know," she said at last, "I don't think she'd interfere. Why, I don't know; but she wouldn't feel that she should. I've only known her two days, but I'm pretty sure that she wouldn't say anything to Father."

"You may be right; Aunt Ione isn't like other people. Perhaps you *are* right about everything. Anyhow, I know I couldn't be unhappier than I am, and even if it didn't help me, at least I'd get away and it would be a comfort to think I'd helped you. Yes, Jan, I'll do it."

"Promise?"

"Honest Injun!" Lydia smiled in the old way, catching her lower lip between her teeth.

They made their final plans and Lydia gave Janet the money she had in her purse. She was writing a letter to Jo when Aunt Ione tapped at the door, said a few words, and went into her own room beyond the girls', closing the door between them. Lydia finished the letter, addressed an envelope, stamped it, and gave it to Janet to mail after the *Phoenix* had sailed. They smiled at each other in confident excitement.

Janet picked up Lydia's hat and tried it on with the veil over her face. She studied her image carefully in the mirror, changing her pose a little and tilting her head to one side, a mannerism characteristic of Lydia. Then she pretended to dabble at her eyes with her handkerchief, hiding their color, already very nearly lost behind the veil.

Lydia, sitting on the edge of the chair by the window, clapped her hands soundlessly.

"You're wonderful!" she breathed. "If you had on my dress, I'd think I was seeing myself," and she began to laugh, and once having begun could not stop again, but went on laughing and choking in her efforts not to be heard in the next room. Janet whipped off the hat and veil and, wetting a towel, wiped Lydia's face until she became quiet. Either Aunt Ione heard nothing, or thought the girls were laughing over some joke. At least, she did not open the door between the rooms until later, when Janet tapped and suggested that they might all go for a walk in the Public Gardens.

That evening at dinner both girls were rather quiet. They had reached a determination which might possibly alter the whole course of their lives, and they were secretly frightened. But great decisions are always frightening. Janet wondered whether Alan would be willing to marry her when she reappeared without so much as a valise—a runaway, whom perhaps even her mother would not dare to take into the home. She would be entirely dependent upon him, and she could not imagine his doing anything but accepting the responsibility, when she had given up everything for his sake. Lydia, too, was deep in her thoughts. Would Jo suddenly find that he loved her when she was gone? Would he miss her? Or would he just be relieved to have her out of the way? A long voyage was like a little death. Would he be angry? He might never forgive her, never take her back when she returned.

Lydia's head went up. Even that would be better than the daily torment of his avoidance; she could not bear it any longer. She had never been able to speak to him about it, but in her letter, she had told him how she felt and why she was leaving; and that she loved him. It was for him to decide whether he wished to say that she had been ill and had gone on a voyage with her father; or to tell their friends that they had separated.

Separated? Her heart felt heavy as a stone. But she could not and would not go on as they were.

Captain Pierce was preoccupied, also, but his thoughts were on professional matters of ladings, and crew, and ships' supplies. He had great confidence in his first mate, Tom Jordan, a young man, but responsible and energetic. The crew was not all signed on yet—the carpenter had been taken ill only that day and two sailors had jumped ship— but Jordan would attend to finding the necessary men. Something had held up the corned beef that had been ordered, but the supply house had sworn it would be at the docks by dawn. Always when a vessel sailed, there were these annoying, last-minute difficulties; if one thing didn't go wrong, another did. The Captain was not unduly disturbed.

Aunt Ione's thoughts may have been on her own affairs, the home at Bristol she was leaving behind; or she may have been remembering how she had once stayed at this same hotel, fifteen years ago, getting ready to sail with her father when she was Janet's age. She had been eager to see the world; not like Janet, miserable and defiant. But then, she had not been beautiful like Janet and in love. Perhaps she thought about Lydia, so talkative, so tense, so ready to praise Jo. But whatever were her thoughts, it was Aunt Ione who, that evening, kept the desultory conversation at dinner easy and social, and later in the hotel parlor continued to lead the talk into safe and happy channels.

At nine o'clock, Captain Pierce drew his watch from his vest pocket, looked at it and suggested that it was bedtime for all hands.

"Breakfast at six," he said. "We sail with the tide a little past eight o'clock. Lydia, my dear, I wish you were going with us."

"Perhaps I shall," said Lydia, laughing. Her father laughed, too.

"Jo Loomis would shoot me when we got back, and I shouldn't blame him. He's a lucky man and he knows it."

"Does he?" asked Lydia archly. She saw Aunt Ione looking at her, and added hastily, "I guess he does. Well, Father, good night and sleep well."

"Good night, Ione, good night, Lydia, good night, Janet."

That night Janet and Lydia, lying side by side, in the big brass bed slept restlessly, and once, waking up, Janet heard Lydia sigh deeply and put her arms about her, saying nothing at all. "How sad life is," she thought. "I never guessed that life was such a sad thing!" And at last they fell asleep.

Once more before the hour of their early rising, Janet woke with a sudden clear realization that something awful had happened. When they had walked in the Public Gardens in the afternoon, she had mailed some letters to her mother and Alan and Susan Mann. Now she was sure that she had mailed Lydia's letter to Jo with them. She had forgotten about Lydia's letter and had merely taken all the envelopes out of her purse and put them into the box without looking at them.

Slipping quietly from bed, she tiptoed through the shadowy room to the bureau and felt about until she found her purse. She opened it softly and searched its depths. At the bottom, Lydia's bills crackled at her touch and she could feel the silver, but there was no letter. For a moment, a surge of panic swept over her. What *had* she done? But then reason, or what appeared to be reason, calmed her. Jo would not get the letter anyway until long after the *Phoenix* sailed. It would be too late for him to do anything. It didn't matter when the letter was mailed, so long as she and Lydia succeeded in their plan. But, more than ever, they must succeed.

CHAPTER VII

The Phoenix Sails

Breakfast, next morning, was an early, silent and hurried meal. Captain Pierce was preoccupied, and the two girls, pale and abstracted. Once more it was Aunt Ione who talked just enough to keep the atmosphere from being tense, her bright blue eyes resting thoughtfully on each of her companions as she spoke.

When the girls, who had eaten little, left the table to see to the closing of Janet's valises, the Captain sat back in his chair watching them as they left the room, and then turned to his sister.

"Janet is behaving better than I expected. Lydia's presence has steadied her. I was afraid there might be tears and hysterics this morning."

Aunt Ione nodded.

"What a lovely creature she is," she contented herself by remarking. The Captain agreed shortly. "And as obstinate as a pig on ice. But she seems to be yielding to the inevitable with better grace than I thought possible."

"Yes, she seems to be, John. I'd better go up and see that my things are in as good order as they seemed to be when I came down to breakfast. Probably I've left out my sponge."

[71]

"Shall I send up for the luggage in five minutes?"

"Say ten. We are well ahead of time."

As Mrs. Pattison came down the upstairs hall, she heard voices from Janet's room, low but vehement.

"Janet! You couldn't have!" Lydia's voice exclaimed distinctly. "You mailed it on purpose to *make* me do it."

"No, really and truly, I didn't. I just forgot it was there."

Then Janet must have heard her aunt's footsteps for her voice subsided, and when Mrs. Pattison tapped and entered, she found her nieces, busy at opposite sides of the room, bent over two valises, both looking upset, and Lydia, at least, angry as well.

"Your father is sending for our things in ten minutes," the older woman said. "Look under the bed and chairs to make sure that nothing has dropped out of sight. I once left my watch under my pillow, and thought that it was gone for good."

In the cab, driving through the Boston streets in the early morning when only a few milk carts were abroad and the sidewalks were nearly deserted and the night's newspapers flapped a little in the breeze, which blew in cool and clean and damp from the harbor, the girls scarcely exchanged a word, though Lydia talked with her father, laughing and chattering as she had when she first arrived at the hotel, while he responded to her gaiety with evident pleasure. Aunt Ione was content to be nearly as silent as Janet, who didn't speak until they had arrived at the wharf and were getting out of the cab. Then, in the confusion, she said in a low voice to her sister, "Please believe me, Lydia."

And this time Lydia, who was never able to keep the white heat of her anger, reached out and squeezed Janet's gloved hand.

[72]

"I do," she whispered, "and anyway it doesn't matter."

Janet crossed the gangplank without a backward glance, and once again the Captain looked relieved. The first mate was at the rail to hand the ladies aboard and the Captain introduced them briefly. It was not a time for much conversation, with so many things to be seen to, but even in that moment, the two girls noticed that Mr. Jordan was young, shy, and had a deep pleasant voice, though he was perhaps too freckled to be considered good-looking. Before the ladies turned to follow a sailor down to their staterooms, they heard the Captain ask, "Has the passenger turned up?" And the mate answered, "Not yet, sir, but his luggage has come aboard."

"I wish people didn't always wait until the last minute," Captain Pierce grumbled. "Well, if he isn't here when the tide turns, we'll put his things ashore and sail without him."

"I didn't know that there was to be another passenger," Janet remarked with surprising interest as she followed her aunt down the steps into the cabin.

"Yes, some young man connected with the owners, I believe," Mrs. Pattison answered over her shoulder.

"Probably Father planned it."

"No, indeed. He was not particularly pleased, but he couldn't very well refuse."

The staterooms opened from the main cabin. Aunt Ione and Janet each had a small one, side by side. As the girls squeezed into Janet's cabin, she whispered teasingly to Lydia.

"You'll have at least two young men to show you around."

"As though I cared!" Lydia whispered back, and then in a rush, "Jan! I can't do it! I simply can't!"

[73]

Aunt Ione looked in at the door.

"I'm going up on deck, girls! You'd better come up soon. There'll be plenty of time to unpack later, Janet."

"Yes, Aunt Ione," both girls exclaimed in chorus, but the moment their aunt had departed, Janet turned to Lydia vehemently.

"Remember what you said about not being able to face it and that you *had* to get away or you'd die? And you promised! You can't change your mind the last minute. We talked it all over yesterday and you wanted to, Lydia."

Lydia sat down on the berth and covered her face with her hands.

"But I'm lonesome for Jo already!" she wailed.

"When you got home, it would all begin again," Janet urged.

Lydia uncovered her hot face and turned brown eyes accusingly upon her sister.

"And now I don't *dare* go home! If only you hadn't sent that letter!"

"I'm sorry, but I did. You'll have to go on with it. Please forgive me."

"Oh, what did I ever come to Boston for!"

But ten minutes later, the two girls appeared on deck together. Lydia's panic had subsided, for the time being at least. She had regained her composure and something of yesterday's mood of decision. The sisters stood beside their aunt, leaning on the rail, watching the frantic activity on the wharf below them. The *Phoenix* was taking on the last of her supplies; drays were being backed up to the edge of the wharf, wives were waving to sailor-husbands, loafers were standing about waiting for the vessel to sail, the owners had come aboard and were talking to the Captain, who answered with his eyes elsewhere, and at any moment, the tug, which was to tow them down the harbor, was due to appear.

"I wonder if the passenger will arrive," Aunt Ione remarked, and, at that moment, there was a great clatter of galloping hoofs and a cab dashed onto the wharf, where a tall, well-dressed young man coolly descended, paid the cabby and strolled towards the gangplank.

"A very telling entrance," Aunt Ione murmured to herself.

Lydia squeezed Janet's arm. The young man's glance had come to rest for a moment on the three ladies above him, passing from Mrs. Pattison's face to Lydia's, and then to Janet's where it rested.

"He admires you," whispered Lydia. "You know he reminds me of someone."

"He looks very romantic," Janet answered indifferently.

The Captain approached with the owners, Mr. Grayson and old Mr. Green, whom he introduced to the ladies of his family.

"And now, Lydia, my dear, it is time to say good-by. These gentlemen have been kind enough to say that they will see you safely to your cab. Remember me to Jo and do write your Mother as soon as you can," and with great affection, he kissed her.

Lydia clung to him and to Aunt Ione, then kissed Janet and made an uncertain step towards the gangway.

"Oh, you've forgotten your purse!" exclaimed Janet in a rather unnatural voice.

"It must be in the stateroom," said Lydia uncertainly.

[75]

"We'll go down and get it."

For a moment Lydia seemed to hang back, but Janet took her arm and both girls disappeared from sight.

They seemed to be gone a rather long time. Captain Pierce took out his watch once or twice and snapped its gold lid open and shut rather impatiently. He was just turning to his sister to suggest that she should hurry up Lydia when the girl appeared alone, her purse in one hand, and dabbling with the other at her eyes.

"Janet's crying so hard she couldn't come up," she gulped. "Good-by, Father dear. Good-by, Aunt Ione."

She, too, was crying so hard that it was not easy to understand what she was saying. The Captain was touched and patted her shoulder as he led her to the gangway.

"There, dear, we'll be back before you know it."

Mr. Grayson offered her his arm with fatherly sympathy, and clinging to it, she was led to a cab, in whose shadows she sat, waving a disconsolate handkerchief as the *Phoenix* left the wharf. Aunt Ione waved back briskly; then, as the tug got underway down the harbor, and the sunlit brick buildings along the wharves wheeled into a new pattern and dropped astern, she returned to the cabin and tapped at her niece's door.

"Janet?" she said softly, "Janet, let me in, dear."

But only sobbing answered her, and, after a while, she went away.

CHAPTER VIII

The Passenger

Mr. Cornelius Sprague was a man who had a gift for getting what he wanted in the world. Nature had given him a trim figure, broad shoulders which carried a coat well, and narrow hips which completed the elegance of his appearance. His face and hands were good, rather bony, but distinguished and full of character. His eyes were a light blue, straightforward but a little mocking. He was courteous from long habit. His handshake and voice were cordial, but his eyes always remained a little aloof.

It was part of his success in life that he knew what he wanted and what he did not want or perhaps no longer wanted. Born in the Sandwich Islands of a missionary family rich in sugar-cane lands and cheap labor, he had known that he wished to go to Harvard, and to enjoy a life in Eastern society. When he had spent three or four seasons in bachelor apartments in New York and Boston, much sought after socially, he knew that he no longer wished to pass his time in amusements, or at least not in amusements alone.

Casting about for his next course, he decided to become the junior partner in his uncle's exporting firm in Shanghai, and if he liked it there, to settle down and get married.

None of the young women with whom he had danced and flirted seemed to him suitable for a life in the Orient. He could afford to wait before taking this step, as he was only twenty-seven years old and in no hurry. This sense of leisure made him decide on a voyage to Shanghai by sailing vessel, instead of attempting to cross the country and take a steamer from San Francisco. Once again he had only to recall his father's cousin, Mr. Henry Grayson of Grayson & Green, owners of the *Phoenix,* and the thing was done.

Standing now by the rail, watching the distant shore, he was well satisfied. The vessel seemed trim, the captain experienced, and he was not displeased to find that there were to be ladies aboard. Just which two ladies he did not know, as he had been in his cabin when one of the girls went ashore. He would know at noon. He hoped it would be the taller one with the copper hair; the other was pretty, too. She reminded him of someone he had met and, methodically, he pursued the memory until he had placed her, though, of course, he might be mistaken.

However, when he came to the cabin that noon, he found only the Captain, the first mate, young Jordan, and Mrs. Pattison, the Captain's sister, waiting for him. Mr. Hinks, the second mate, ordinarily dined later. A place had been set for someone beside Mrs. Pattison, but the steward removed it at a word from the Captain. Nothing was said, and later at dinner, the same thing happened. This time, Cornelius Sprague's curiosity was definitely aroused. It was not rough, he reasoned; surely this young lady could not feel ill. Was she to remain in seclusion during the entire voyage? Was she an invalid? She had not looked like an invalid in the glimpse he had had of her.

After supper, finding himself alone in the cabin with

[78]

Mrs. Pattison, he waited until she looked up from the book she was reading, to ask her what it was.

"Scott's *Antiquary*," she said, laying it aside. "It is one of my favorites."

"But do you read novels?" he rallied her. "I had imagined that you would read only improving books."

"Why?"

"Aren't you a missionary, ma'am?"

"My husband was. That's a very different matter."

"Perhaps your niece is going to be a missionary?"

"Oh, no."

"Miss Pierce *is* your niece, isn't she?"

"Oh, yes."

There was a slight silence, then, unrebuffed, the young man tried again.

"You know, when I was coming aboard I thought I recognized one of the young ladies. She looked very much like a bride I met several times in Boston, a young Mrs. Loomis; she and her husband knew some of the same people I knew."

"Really?" Mrs. Pattison's tone was as noncommittal as ever, but now he felt that she was listening to him. He was a little annoyed by her reticence, and although his tone remained perfectly polite, it was not without intention that he made his next remark.

"Like your niece, she was very pretty, but, unlike her, I am sure, she was such a goose that she had made herself and her husband a laughing stock. She overdid her part of the loving wife, and wouldn't let her husband out of her sight for a moment. If he so much as stood up to look out of a window, she joined him; their friends were much amused."

"Indeed?" asked Mrs. Pattison. "The world is full of foolish and malicious people."

He could not tell from her tone whether or not her remark was intended to be merely general. As though the conversation had come to an end, she reached for the book on the table, but he forestalled her. He had yielded, perhaps unwisely, to his temper, but he was too much a man of the world to wish to antagonize a lady whom he was to see daily—yes, hourly—for the next four or five months. Now he laid himself out to be charming and attentive. He stopped asking questions and instead entertained her with accounts of the theatre and opera, the differences between New York and Boston society, and amusing incidents at Saratoga and Newport. She listened to him intelligently, now and then making some suitable remark. When the Captain came in, he found the two in the midst of a lively conversation and dropped into the seat by the table with an air of satisfaction.

"This seems homelike," he said. "We haven't sailed together, Ione, since we were children. Do you remember how quiet we had to be because one mate or another seemed always off duty and sleeping? Silence was a rule Father enforced."

Mrs. Pattison laughed.

"Yes. Do you remember all the games we learned to play by holding up our fingers? And someone taught us to talk the deaf and dumb language. In those days, captains' children were seen but not heard on board ship."

Soon the Captain excused himself and went out again, and Mrs. Pattison rose at the same time, saying good night pleasantly. Cornelius Sprague had no doubts but that he had made an ally.

During the night, the *Phoenix* ran into headwinds and by morning the ship was rolling and pitching uncomfortably. It was on such a day that a lady passenger might well keep her cabin, but as the company gathered for breakfast with the Captain, the door of Janet's cabin opened, and a girl stepped out.

Mrs. Pattison turned white and then gave a sharp sigh of relief as she saw who it was, but the others took the newcomer for granted.

"Good morning, Janet," said the Captain.

"Good morning, Father. Good morning, Aunt Ione. Good morning, Mr. Jordan," Janet murmured, quickly taking her seat beside her aunt as standing was difficult in the lurching cabin. The racks were on the table to keep the dishes from sliding. The Captain introduced Mr. Sprague.

"We have been hoping that you were not indisposed, Miss Pierce," the young man remarked, and she answered gravely.

"Oh, not at all, thank you. I think I am going to be a good sailor."

"I believe we can find a dry spot for the chairs, Janet, if it doesn't blow up any harder; but you had better wear a cloak. It's windy on deck," her father said.

The Captain did not appear to have more than glanced at his daughter, but he had received a very surprising impression. She had left Thomaston a girl and sometime during the past week she had become a woman. Serenity had taken the place of the joyousness he had seen in her face on the day of his return, and her features had a fine clear-cut sense of line rather than the glow which had permeated them. Captain Pierce sighed to himself as he folded his napkin, for the first time doubting the wisdom of his course.

[81]

Had the sacrifice been too great for the gain? Certainly it was too late to reconsider now.

But Janet fitted well into life aboard ship. After that day alone in her room, when it had seemed impossible to believe that she was actually being taken away from Alan, she had faced facts squarely. Poor Lydia she had not blamed. At the last moment, she would not and could not leave Jo. If only that wretched letter had not been sent!

Janet's own experience with letters was better. Among her things she found a note tucked into the folds of a dress.

"Do not give up hope. Your friends here will be active. We will keep an eye on what goes on and report everything to you."

The scrawl was a small thing to have comforted her, but it did. Dear Steve! It warmed her heart to think that somebody—if only a young brother—was on her side. She had made every effort, twisting and turning like a fish in a net, but here she was. Now she would make the best of it, since there was nothing more that she could do.

Janet found that she was a natural sailor. She had never been to sea before and had had no way of measuring the attraction that a vessel on its course would hold for her. The salt smells, the great wash of the waves, the smoky tossing horizons, the cloud-drifted skies, and the *Phoenix* itself, so tensely alive in the midst of all these forces, enthralled her. One morning, she placed her hand on the mainmast in passing and was thrilled to feel the vibration which ran through it. She liked to watch Mr. Jordan and Mr. Hinks, the second mate, taking observations at noon; she liked the shouted orders and the "Aye, aye, sir," of the sailors; she could have sat back in her chair for hours, content to see the sails swaying against the sky.

Slowly the color came back to her cheeks and the brightness to her eyes and the life to her windblown hair. She would stand at the prow of the *Phoenix* for half a morning, looking out at the pathless and moving waste before her, thinking of Alan. Everything reminded her of him.

On meeting Cornelius Sprague, she had thought that he was very handsome, but since it was not in Alan's way, his good looks had left her unmoved; she considered him agreeable to talk to and he helped to pass an hour not otherwise occupied, but that was all. Then one sunny day as she was sitting with Aunt Ione, with Matty, the ship's maltese cat, at her feet, lulled by the peace of a day almost completely calm and the faint hiss of small waves against the ship's sides, Janet glanced towards the prow and saw Alan leaning against the rail.

His back was turned towards her. There were the broad shoulders, the well-set neck and the swirl of hair at the crown of the head which she knew so well. So overwhelming was the impression that Janet half rose from her chair, startling the cat, and uttering an exclamation at which the figure turned. But instantly Alan vanished, and it was Cornelius Sprague who hurried to her side.

"Are you unwell, Miss Pierce? Is there anything I can do for you? May I bring you something?"

"It's the heat," she said, "All at once it came over me. Would you be kind enough, Mr. Sprague, to bring me one of the palm leaf fans from the cabin?"

By the time he returned, Janet, fully recovered, was chatting with her aunt, and Matty had resumed her nap between the two chairs. But from that moment, Janet's calm manner towards Cornelius became a little self-conscious, and now she blushed sometimes when she talked with him, and her eyes turned away from his. Aunt Ione noticed the change and spoke of it to Captain Pierce.

"Have you observed Janet with Mr. Sprague recently? I think that she is falling in love with him, on the rebound, as people call it."

"It might be a good thing," said the Captain. "I know his father and uncle. The young man belongs to a very successful family and will succeed, though he has given himself a long gentleman's holiday before beginning."

"Perhaps I'm wrong." Aunt Ione frowned a little. "Don't say anything to her, whatever you do."

"I should be unlikely to."

Cornelius, too, was inclined to interpret Janet's change of manner in the same way and felt a good deal of staisfaction in consequence. Often when he came up to chat with the ladies, he found Janet still shining as it were with a reflected happiness, her old indifferent serenity gone, and her ready tongue unsure of itself.

"What a silly schoolgirl I must seem," she thought after some inept rejoinder. "Still, it doesn't matter two beans what he thinks about me."

It never occurred to her that anyone could find her attractive in her new awkwardness and confusions. She wondered sometimes why Cornelius Sprague didn't give her up for a fool and keep away from her. Probably he felt sorry for her, she decided. Certainly he seemed to be always at her side.

CHAPTER IX

Shipboard

AT THE end of three weeks at sea, the *Phoenix* entered the area of the trade winds and work aboard ship grew easier for everyone. For days at a time, the vessel sailed under the same canvas; there was little going aloft necessary and even Mr. Jordan, the first mate, had more free time on his hands. Often now he would stop beside Janet if he found her alone or with her aunt and say a few words to her.

One day a small bird appeared in the rigging; Mr. Jordan caught it and brought it, cupped in his hands, to Janet.

"It's exhausted," he said. "We must be nearly a hundred miles offshore and it's lost its course; some kind of warbler, isn't it?"

Janet knew little about birds.

"I guess so," she said. "Will it live? See how bright its eyes are and it doesn't act afraid."

"I suppose we seem a great wonder to it," the man pondered, looking down at the bird in his hands. "Sailors consider a bird in the rigging unlucky, but when I was a boy, I raised several young birds I found out of the nest. One I had for two or three years, and it would fly after me wherever I went."

The carpenter made a little cage for the bird, and during this halcyon weather it hung out on deck beyond Matty's reach. The sow in her pen between the starboard boats farrowed and there were eleven amusing little pigs, three black and the rest spotted. The two sheep were in a pen on the opposite side of the deck and sometimes when Janet awakened and heard their bleating, she would forget for a moment where she was and think that she was fifteen again and at home, hearing Steve's pet lamb calling for breakfast.

These quiet days, with talk and sewing beside Aunt Ione on the after deck, with strolls beside Cornelius Sprague, and sometimes a little singing to the guitar he had brought with him among his voluminous luggage, with hours when Mr. Jordan attempted to teach her navigation, all had a tranquil domesticity about them that was good for Janet. Not that she forgot Alan; far from it! But she ceased to struggle, and lived in the present again. The *Phoenix* was a small world, surrounded by the illimitable seas, and slowly its interests took possession of her. When one day they found the *Seven Brothers* of Philadelphia on their course, she shared the silent excitement of all aboard as to which vessel could outsail the other. Up went every sail and for hours the two tacked along side by side, company makers, a mile or so apart, the gentle trade wind in their canvas and the sea curling white at their bows. When the sun went down, the *Seven Brothers* was a little ahead, but at dawn, she was still in sight.

"Father," Janet said at breakfast, "you *mustn't* let her beat us."

"We're not going to, if we can help it," the Captain answered smiling, "but the *Phoenix* sails better with a little more wind. We'll have to wait. You might try whistling when you go up on deck."

Mr. Jordan, who had been on the night watch, was having breakfast with the others before turning in.

"Come up on deck with me, Miss Pierce, and we'll whistle for a wind in a way that *must* be obeyed," he said.

Cornelius Sprague remarked lazily, "You'd better be careful, Miss Janet, you're witch enough as it is."

Janet smiled and flushed a little. She never knew just how to take the worldly compliments, which seemed part of his conversation. The mate, who had finished breakfast, excused himself and went on deck. Janet forgot about his offer, but when she appeared, he was waiting for her.

"Ready?" he asked.

She could see the *Seven Brothers*, a pillar of white sail, like a lighthouse above the sea to the southeast. The air smelled delicious; the soft light breeze touched her cheek. Her father was standing near by and she said almost gaily, "Do you encourage my taking part in magic ceremonies, Father?"

"Certainly," he answered in the same tone, "if you can call up a wind. We can't let Philadelphia show us her heels."

"So," said Mr. Jordan, "you are duly authorized. Step with me to the mainmast, Miss Pierce, if you please."

"I'd better go along to see that no black magic takes place," put in Cornelius Sprague, offering Janet his arm; but Tom Jordan eyed him firmly.

"I'm sorry, sir, but the wind will not answer if more than two take part in the ceremony."

Mr. Sprague's face stiffened but he said, pleasantly enough, "Oh, in that case, of course I withdraw."

[87]

When Janet stood beside the mainmast, she put out her hand as she always did to feel the quiver of life that seemed to run through the wood, as though it and the ship were living things.

"Now, whistle," commanded Mr. Jordan, and Janet gave a good clear-cut whistle, ending with an upward note like a schoolboy whistling for his dog.

"Fine," said the mate, smiling at her, "the wind ought to hear that. But to make sure, take this and stick it as deep in the mast as you can," and he handed her his sailor's knife.

She had a moment's unwillingness, as though she might really hurt something alive if she obeyed him; but she overcame her reluctance, took the knife and struck strongly at the mast before her. The point of the blade entered into the pine an inch or two and when she let go, the knife hung suspended in the air, vibrating strongly. No sap flowed from the gash as the girl half expected, watching the mast uneasily.

"We will leave it there until the wind comes," said the mate. "It won't be your fault if we don't have a good breeze in the next few hours. Thank you, Miss Pierce; and now I'll go below and catch up on my sleep before the wind strikes us."

Janet went back to the after deck where Mr. Sprague tried to teach her to play chess. The *Phoenix* idled along through an idle sea, and now and then a flying fish sped from the sapphire waters, through which they moved, up into the air like a shining apparition.

At the end of the first hour, Cornelius Sprague remarked, "Where's the breeze you were calling for, Miss Janet?"

"Wait and see," she laughed, but she herself expected

nothing. Yet at about eleven o'clock, she felt the air stirring more coolly past her cheek, and the vessel began to stir and creak; looking up, she saw the sails growing taut, and felt the deck tilt a little beneath her feet, and heard, half unconsciously, a difference in the hiss and splash of the water along the ship's side.

"Why, the wind's come!" she exclaimed, astonished and rather awed.

Somehow she did not think that her companion looked altogether pleased, but her father, going by a few minutes later, stopped to pat her cheek.

"You've done very well for a novice," he said jestingly. "Now let the *Seven Brothers* look out!"

"It's probably only a capful," Cornelius Sprague suggested, but Captain Pierce shook his head.

"No, usually in this latitude if a wind comes up, it holds steady for some hours at the least. We'll hope so, anyhow."

Perhaps Janet had driven the knife—now back in its sheath—too far into the mast, for that afternoon when the Captain was below deck and the first mate was on duty, a sudden squall appeared off at sea, ruffling the water in a catspaw of running darkness. Mr. Jordan ordered the topsails reefed and half-a-dozen men were in the rigging when the wind struck. The *Phoenix* heeled suddenly. After the days of dreamlike sailing, the jar was unaccustomed and came sooner than it had been expected.

Everything happened at once. There was a cry from the topsail yards and a body came pitching downwards through the air and struck the water beyond the rail. The waves closed over it. Several voices shouted, "Man overboard!" The mate ran to a grating and threw it towards where the sailor had last been seen. The man at the wheel brought the vessel into the wind with a jerk which almost hurled the ladies out of their chairs, and Cornelius Sprague, standing at the rail, climbed over it and dived into the sea.

CHAPTER X

The Rescue

THE next few minutes were ones that Janet would never wish to live over again. Somehow she found herself at the rail, looking back at the wash of the ship where two heads appeared and disappeared like bobbing corks, one much more often seen than the other.

"What a good swimmer he is!" Aunt Ione's voice exclaimed at her elbow, and the girl became aware that Cornelius was moving strongly towards the other man, who was floundering about in a losing fight to keep his head above the water. The waves were not high; the squall had passed as quickly as it had come, and could now be seen in the distance like a cloud-shadow over the sea. It had scarcely disturbed the surface in passing, but the long swells had been broken by the keel of the *Phoenix*, and it was in those disturbed waters that the sailor was struggling to keep afloat until help could come. All the time the vessel was drifting away, but Janet could hear Mr. Jordan's shouted orders, the creaking of the davits as a boat was lowered, and a protesting bleat or two from the sheep.

Now Cornelius Sprague had reached the grating and was pushing it ahead of him towards the drowning man; but the other was too far gone even to see it. His hands went up, then hands and head disappeared. In a quick flurry of powerful strokes, the passenger left the grating and swam to the spot where the other had gone down.

"Careful now, careful," breathed Aunt Ione, "better one than two."

But now both figures reappeared, struggling together; both disappeared and reappeared nearer the grating.

"He keeps his head," Aunt Ione murmured.

"Oh, why *doesn't* the boat come?" cried Janet, not even aware that the boat had left the ship's side and was being rowed at top speed towards the men in the water; but before it had covered half the distance, Cornelius Sprague had succeeded in getting his hand on the grating and in hauling his companion to its edge, to which the man now clung.

A few minutes later, the rescue was completed by Mr. Hinks in charge of the ship's boat, while Janet anxiously twisted her handkerchief until she had torn it to bits; for getting two men—one half unconscious—into the boat was no easy matter, even in a comparatively calm sea, and at any moment, she dreaded to see the tender capsized and all flung into the water together.

But she need not have been afraid. Both men were pulled over the gunwale, the sailor first, and the grating was made fast with a line and hauled back to the *Phoenix*. Captain Pierce had hurried up on deck and was there when the men came aboard. The sailor was helped below to hot blankets and his fill of rum, but Cornelius Sprague came aboard with something of a swagger.

"Now, you see what happens when you dabble in magic," he said jestingly to Janet as he passed her on his way to his cabin to change his clothes. He was in high good humor with himself and the world. Captain Pierce came up to shake his wet hand and to thank him, and all the sailors stood grinning respectfully about him.

"It's nothing, sir," Cornelius Sprague protested, "I knew that few seamen can swim and I merely thought it well to see that the fellow reached the grating, which someone kindly made available."

"Not many men would have succeeded," the Captain replied warmly. "But get off your wet clothes before you catch cold. This mild air is deceptive."

As Cornelius went below to his cabin, the Captain glanced along the skyline to where the *Seven Brothers* appeared, somewhat larger than she had been a few hours before.

"Get the *Phoenix* underway, mister!" he said sharply to the first mate. "We can't stand here idling while that Philadelphian sails off with her nose in the air!"

If Janet's father could turn his thoughts so quickly from the rescue to the race, it was more than Janet could manage. She sat in a kind of daze, reliving the last half-hour from the moment when the *Phoenix* had keeled over before the squall. Mr. Sprague had certainly been wonderful, risking his life for a stranger. She saw him in that instant at the rail, outlined against the sky, and then she saw his head moving forward under the powerful impetus of his swimming and relived his struggle in saving the drowning man.

And, for once, she was not comparing him with Alan, nor even thinking of Alan.

The breeze which had come to them held, and three days later, the *Phoenix* drew up on the *Seven Brothers*, and after an hour's tense struggle, passed her. On the fifth day, the sails of the other vessel twinkled like a far-off white star

[93]

and disappeared from sight. Then they struck rough weather and, forty-five days out from Boston, crossed the equator and ran into southeast winds, against which they tacked and tacked until Janet was tired of getting nowhere. Two weeks later, they neared Cape Horn and the weather turned cold and the winds were uncertain. Albatrosses circled their masts, appearing like ghosts out of the fog. For days at a time, the officers could not take observations and the ship had to sail by dead reckoning. Instead of rain, hail beat on the decks and froze along the yardarms, and the *Phoenix* rolled so that, on several occasions, the galley fire had to be put out and the tired officers and crew were denied even the comfort of hot coffee when they came below, beating their cold hands together.

At night, the ship often had to lie to and rolled so that Janet was nearly thrown out of her bunk, and could not sleep. The food by now was hard to eat; the biscuits were weevily and the salt beef disgusting to their palates. One of the sheep was killed and the fresh mutton put heart into everyone. Then, after nearly two weeks, a fine day broke and they could see the rocky coast on whose reefs so many ships had been wrecked. The Straits of Le Maire opened before them and, early in the morning under a red sun, they entered them, and by eight o'clock, were nearly in Good Success Bay; but a west wind came up and by afternoon, the *Phoenix* was lying to once more, with the main and mizzen topsails set under close reef. Continual west winds faced them, and day after day, they fought to hold their position or to gain a little headway when the wind let up for an hour. Half the little pigs had been washed overboard or crushed in the gales. Janet mourned for them—poor land creatures taken to sea by no will of their own.

[94]

On many days she and Aunt Ione were not allowed to go up on deck. They sat precariously in the cabin, on chairs bolted to the floor, and moved cautiously—when at all—so as not to be flung across the room and against the walls or furniture. Neither Janet nor her aunt was sick, but the days were endless and rather frightening.

"Why in the world does anyone go to sea?" she asked the first mate one day as they sat down to another meal, this time of dried fish and bread; he smiled at her from a face gray with weariness.

"It's this that makes the trade winds interesting. Keep up heart. It won't be much longer."

Janet's father brought the ladies such books as he had. They were mostly treatises on navigation, but there were among them several worn copies of Scott's novels, and the stories of Fenimore Cooper. Aunt Ione, too, had a few more recent books with her, so they spent their time in reading until their eyes ached; and then they went to lie down, holding themselves wedged in their bunks so that they would not be thrown out.

Sometimes Cornelius Sprague attempted to entertain them, but, in the stuffy rolling cabin, it was impossible to play any game, and conversation soon died out. Most days, Janet could not write letters nor keep her diary, and her thoughts became vague, and she seldom dreamed about her future; even Alan seemed far away.

Then after twenty-two days, the *Phoenix* crossed latitude 50°, longitude 85° and was officially around the Cape. A few days later, good weather set in and all hands were busy making repairs, mending sails and splicing lines, and putting patches of new wood in the deck where the old had been splintered by the pounding of the waves. Janet celebrated by

baking cookies and two apple pies, which were warmly welcomed at the table. Water was getting low and was so stale by
now that Janet drank little of it, but, fortunately, a tail wind
sent them speeding up the mountainous coast of South America. One night, rain fell, and the casks could be filled again,
and Aunt Ione and Janet were again allowed to wash out a
few of their things.

Then one of the sailors fell sick and Captain Pierce feared
that he might have scurvy.

"But we shall be putting in at Lima for fresh supplies and
mail," he assured the ladies. "All he needs is fruit and something green. It hasn't got hold of him yet."

At Lima, the agent brought the mail out to the *Phoenix* in
the harbor boat and Janet slipped off to her stateroom to
read her letters. She had a packet from her mother and Steve
and her school friends. Rather to her surprise, there were one
or two letters addressed in Alex Hunt's handwriting. But it
was Alan's that she sought, shuffling through the others
hungrily until she had found the three or four thin envelopes
that were his. But when she had torn them open and read the
letters, she was secretly a little bewildered by them. After the
fierce discipline of the Cape and the long leisures of the
trades, his letters seemed singularly pointless and insipid.
What had happened to him—or to her?

She was a woman reading a boy's letters. It was not that the
greatness of the sea dwarfed the affairs of a little town like
Thomaston; when she read her mother's letters or even
Alex Hunt's, the news of her friends and acquaintances
seemed still important; but she looked to Alan's words to
feed her spirit, and found nothing but a few scattered phrases
of casual affection and a schoolboy's carping at the various
jobs he had successively tried, but which either bored him or

[96]

worked him too hard. He had tried clerking at his mother's cousin's store, but old John Beale expected him to stay three nights a week until nine, so he had left there, too, and now Alex Hunt had the job. He might get a place at Flo's father's bank, even though the old man was sick at home, but he thought he'd rather go shares with Ben Hascomb with his traps; already Ben had caught five foxes. "The first good fox fur I get, I'll save for a muff for you."

Janet stared ahead at the cabin wall. It might be Steve writing! A boy at the Academy might join that no-account Ben Hascomb for a season, but anyone knew you couldn't make a living that way! John Beale was looking for a young man to take over his store. If only Alan had buckled down to work for a few years, it would have been his. But now, Alex had it, and Alex would keep it. She thought of the restrained power in Alex. He was a man you could pin to, even at eighteen.

Steve wrote in his usual elaborate way:

> "We've got F. under observation and so far she is not dangerous. A. is sidestepping, but more and more often, he gets caught. Will inform you if anything serious takes place, and will take whatever steps may seem necessary at the time."

Janet laughed ruefully. "F." must be Flo, she supposed; but the boys were foolish to think that Alan would ever fall for Flo's obvious coquetries. Everyone laughed at her—Alan most of all. Her mother's letters were tender and gentle, filled with accounts of the children; of how much better Steve was doing at school—"and he's beginning to pay some attention to girls. I hear he walked home with Sue Danvers last week and stayed for a candy-pull, but he didn't say anything to me about it"—of how much she missed Janet. And the girls wrote of parties and engagements, with exclamations of envy: "Oh, Janet, you must be having such a wonderful time! I wish I were in your shoes!"

There was a letter from Lydia, too; and this Janet opened last, fearful of what it might say. How *had* she faced Jo when she got home, knowing that he had already read her letter of farewell? But when Janet got up her courage to read Lydia's letter, she found no mention of that return home and no outward sign of unhappiness. Perhaps she was concealing her feelings as she had the first day at the Parker House.

Janet read the letter again.

"It sounds all right," she decided doubtfully, and returned to Alan's correspondence, hoping that on second reading, it would seem different. But in vain did she look for some heartwarming sentence, some grown-up expression of opinion, even some young endearing jest. The letters were dull. That was the truth, though she could not admit it, least of all to herself. She put them away with the others and, instead, thought about him—of his looks, his voice, his arms about her. That was the real Alan, the Alan she would hold to. But all the time they were at Lima, Janet went about in a chastened and subdued mood.

The voyage to San Francisco passed almost without incident. They made only thirty or thirty-five miles on most days, but the *Phoenix* was again provisioned and at last they picked up the Farallons in the early morning and the pilot came aboard. Captain Pierce immediately asked if the *Seven Brothers* had arrived, but hearing that she had not been sighted, he appeared satisfied.

For a week, they anchored in the harbor off the city discharging and taking on cargo, and every day Cornelius

Sprague went ashore with the ladies, sight-seeing and taking them to dine at the elaborate hotels of the city. Aunt Ione had friends in San Francisco who also entertained them, and the days passed quickly.

They sailed out through the Golden Gate one sunny morning and dropped anchor at Honolulu just two weeks later. Here, Cornelius Sprague surprised everyone, including himself, by deciding to join his family for a few months before proceeding to China. While the *Phoenix* lay in the harbor, he entertained the Captain and the two ladies at his parents' great house in the shadow of Diamond Head, and on the day they were to put out to sea, he escorted Janet to the shore with his arms filled with leis of fresh flowers for her to wear.

"Let me put them over your head," he said, drawing her a little to one side. "There's something I want to say to you, Miss Janet."

"I must be getting to the boat, I'm afraid. Aunt Ione's looking for me now."

"Wait a minute. A minute won't matter. I've got to say it before you leave. I know that your heart is engaged just now and, I, too, have not settled down to my career. But next year, things will be different for us both, and, then, if all goes well, I shall speak again."

Janet was so accustomed to think of Cornelius Sprague as a man of the world and incapable of being seriously interested in her that she really did not understand his meaning.

"Speak about what?" she asked, beginning to walk towards the boat where the others were clustered, apparently waiting for her.

But Cornelius stopped her with a hand on each shoulder, turning her around to meet his eyes.

[99]

"About marriage, you little goose!" he burst out and, leaning down, kissed her full on the mouth.

She looked at him incredulously.

"Oh, you shouldn't have done that! I'm in love with somebody else."

"And next year you may be in love with me!"

Then he let her go, and she walked down to the beach beside him in silence, blushing and trembling a little.

No one seemed to have noticed anything out of the way, though Tom Jordan looked more serious than usual. Captain Pierce shook hands with Cornelius warmly; Aunt Ione made her kind, noncommittal adieux, and Janet raised her head on her long neck, ringed and garlanded with flowers, to stammer her good-by.

As the distance between the boat and the shore widened, Aunt Ione, waving her handkerchief to the figure on the beach, said to her niece, over her shoulder,

"Wave, Janet."

And Janet, with a start, raised her right hand and waved to Cornelius Sprague.

CHAPTER XI

The Journey Begins

WHEN the anchor was weighed and the high mountains of the islands dropped slowly out of sight below the horizon and the last birds turned from following the *Phoenix,* life on board ship settled down again to its daily routine. For the ladies, it was somewhat quieter than it had been and they realized how often Cornelius Sprague's talk, or some game of his suggesting had helped to pass an eventless morning or a dragging afternoon. Janet found herself thinking of him more often than pleased her, and for some days, she would turn at the sound of footsteps, expecting to see him, and would feel a wave almost of loss when she realized that he was far away. A memory of those last minutes, of love-making that was scarcely love-making, kept returning to her as she sat looking dreamily out to the long Pacific rollers. When he saw her again, he would really woo her—if he still wished to! She wondered what he would say, what he would do, provided, always, that he cared to say or do anything at all when the time came. She remembered what energy and daring he had shown when the man had fallen overboard. No wonder that there was a certain not unbecoming arrogance latent behind all his good manners.

Then she would give herself a little shake and turn to talk

to Aunt Ione or to read the book on her lap or to see if the steward were in a good enough humor to let her make a cake. He was the master of the galley, and the Captain's orders were that no one was so much as to enter his domain except on his invitation. But that was usually not hard to obtain, especially now when the ship was stocked with fresh supplies and his temper was not tested by his having almost nothing to put on the table but bread made from weevily flour and corned beef and salted pork or fish.

Whatever the young gentleman from Honolulu might wish from Janet (provided he wished anything) he would meet with a steadfast refusal. Her heart was otherwise engaged; but she passed more than one pleasant hour making up imaginary conversations between them, all ending, "But as it is, my answer must be 'No'!"

After the first few days of adjustment to Cornelius' absence, the voyage took on a new pattern. The Captain stopped more often to talk with his sister and daughter, and Janet grew to know her father in a new way. She had seen him only at home between trips as the beloved head of the house and yet a stranger. Here, she saw him at his work, carrying on his shoulders the responsibility for the vessel and for everyone aboard her, intimately concerned with each detail of each day's happenings, and yet always acting through the agency of the mates, so that he retained a certain remoteness from the crew and remained the embodiment of authority. She saw him in the long calms that beset them and in storm when, for forty-eight hours at a time, he would never take the clothes off his back nor sleep for more than an hour or two at a stretch.

And, in spite of the sense of wrong which she had felt when she came aboard against her will, she was forced to judge him as courageous and enduring in his dealings with nature and just in his dealings with men.

Her manner imperceptibly changed, taking on its old warmth and pride in him, and he, in his turn, now treated her with open affection. The three on the after deck were actually a family group again, and more and more often Tom Jordan would linger when off duty to sit and talk with them or to play chequers with Janet or her aunt. His coming never made the girl's heart skip a beat. It seemed as though she had always known him, always liked and trusted him, but, as the days went on, she depended more and more upon him for youthful companionship. The second mate, Ted Hinks, was a gray-haired, taciturn man with a wall-eye, married and with four children. He believed that women, like birds, aboard ship brought bad luck, and as the *Phoenix* now carried not only one woman but two and a bird as well—for the warbler had managed to live even through the awful fortnight of circling the Horn—he glumly retired into himself, did his duty and waited for the worst to happen.

When at last they reached Yokohama and Kobe, Shanghai and Hongkong, it was Tom Jordan who took Janet about to see the sights in the intervals between unloading and loading cargoes. These new worlds were intoxicating to Janet, to ride in a rickshaw or palanquin to pagodas and temples, to drink tea by pools filled with gold fish in gardens of curiously shaped stones, to go shopping for silks and brocades and ivory and shell ornaments through narrow streets filled with people of another race, all these were a never-ending delight to her. In several ports, Aunt Ione had missionary friends, at whose homes the ladies visited, and it was pleasant to sleep in beds again and to walk across stationary floors after so many months on the sea.

They were on their way up the coast of China again and had stopped at Fusan in Korea, taking on a final consignment, when Captain Pierce received word at his agents' which necessitated his return to Shanghai.

"Oh, dear, and we were headed for home!" exclaimed Janet. "What a pity! But at least we'll have a chance to see Mr. Sprague and the fine Chinese house he writes about. We missed him on the way down to Hongkong in the fall."

"We got there before him," said the Captain. "I saw his uncle; in fact, did business with him. I've known him now for some years. It's a fine family. Cornelius has taken his time to buckle down to work, but once he gets started, he'll make a success. That young man, for all his society manners, is intelligent and ambitious to an unusual degree."

"And obstinate as a mule," added Aunt Ione, "Not that obstinacy mayn't be a good thing in its place."

"He's not as nice as Alan," Janet spoke up rather weakly, and her father laughed and patted her hand.

"What do you hear from the boy?" he asked indulgently. "Doing anything yet to earn a living?"

Janet flushed. "He's going to help his uncle on his farm this summer. That horrible Ben Hascomb cheated him out of his share of the skins they'd trapped," she added defensively.

"Anyone who trusted Hascomb might expect to be skinned with the rest," the Captain argued with perfect good humor. "But I don't see Alan as a farmer."

"He was quite interested last summer."

"He'd better get a job with a future. What do you hear of Flo Andrews? Mother writes that they're seen together a good deal."

Janet's head went up and she smiled brilliantly.

"He's written me about that. Flo's always been after him,

[104]

but Alan wouldn't be interested in her if she were the last girl left on earth."

Actually she herself had been having reports from Steve, giving dates and further details of the meetings which had taken place between Alan and Flo. The boys had been keeping an eye on everything, and once Alan had seen them and pursued them, and they had barely escaped into Millard's house, slamming and bolting the back door in his face. Janet did not pay much attention to Steve's revelations, but a cautious reference in one of Susan Mann's letters she took more seriously.

"But actually," she argued to herself, "Alan can't stay home doing nothing all the time I'm gone. He's got to go somewhere and see someone, and of course Flo is always asking him; but there's no one he's safer with," and, to reassure herself, she went to the little mirror in her cabin and looked at her face, which looked back at her with a radiant youthfulness which even Thomaston had never seen. She did not herself realize that it was no longer quite a girl's face which was mirrored there, nor quite a girl's eyes which looked into hers. Nearly a year had gone by, a year of thinking and feeling and growing, a year of living both intensely and a little aloofly, set far off from her past. It had changed and deepened and perfected her, but all that she realized was that Alan would still find her pretty. And thinking of Flo's harsh voice and squat figure, she felt only a slight uneasiness and could answer her father now with almost complete assurance.

But already the Captain had left the subject and turned to his sister. "Ione, I think you and Janet might go up into the mountains where you and Richard used to spend your summers. It's late May now and I don't think we can get back from Shanghai until late June or early July. You might as well have a few weeks ashore and show Janet something of the world you know so well."

Aunt Ione didn't answer at once but her bright blue eyes searched her brother's face.

"Is there any sickness in Shanghai?" she asked.

The Captain paused a moment before he replied.

"It's early for sickness," he said. "Don't worry about us. But I'd like you two to see a little of the world when the opportunity offers. You'll be glad to get off ship for awhile. I'll keep an eye on that bird of yours, Janet, or rather young Jordan will, if Mr. Hinks doesn't wring its neck."

"He wouldn't dare!" Janet began indignantly, but then she saw that her father was teasing her. For a moment, when Aunt Ione had spoken of sickness on the coast, she had been terribly worried, but she was quite reassured by her father's answer, especially as Aunt Ione seemed satisfied and said nothing more.

The very next morning, Mrs. Pattison went briskly ashore and began hiring men until she had nineteen or twenty, mostly elderly grandfathers with thin gray mustaches and whiskers like philosophers in a Chinese painting, their wiry frames bundled in soiled white trousers and coats, their heads covered with high transparent hats, of black woven horsehair, which tied under their chins. Only the cook, Tsu, who was also to be number one man, was younger. He had lived with a missionary family, could speak some English and showed by his clothes a Western influence.

Once the necessary men had been decided upon, Aunt Ione began a competent purchase of supplies. Mr. Cochrane, who was a merchant in the town and acted as agent for a good many American firms, gladly lent two folding cot-beds and two carrying chairs for the trip, and in a few days everything was ready. The *Phoenix* took the whole expedition on board and dropped them late the next day in a small harbor, the point of departure for the mountains. With a sinking heart, Janet watched the well-known sails make out again to sea. The *Phoenix* had been the bridge to home always, in storm and calm, and now she was gone and, yes, young Mr. Jordan was gone, with that anxious look on his face and a final hard press of her hand.

"Take care of yourself," he had said, coming back up the shingle to say it.

But as she sat in her carrying chair, with a white-clad carrier in front and one behind, walking through rice fields where little green frogs with bright coral bellies croaked at their passing, she began to take an interest in the world about her again.

It was exciting to be with Aunt Ione, on their own, in this long line of carriers and jiggy-men strung out single file on the narrow path between the fields, headed towards those high mountains of pointed stone, which rose in an apparently unbroken wall above the flat coastal plain. They were to stay that night at a native inn which Aunt Ione knew, and next day they would climb Sleeping Dog Pass, and by night they should be at the Lower Monastery where they would stay. There would be no one around them but Koreans; no one to talk to but one another or the monks through Aunt Ione, who knew the language, or Tsu with his checked cap and vest and American shoes, which lent a bizarre touch to his white Korean clothes. They would be shut in by these mountains like enormous screens of stone. "How unreal it all seems!" Janet thought. "Like an adventure in a dream," and as they moved slowly towards that line of blue, towering pinnacles, she felt a mounting excitement seizing her.

CHAPTER XII

Tiger

At noon the next day, Janet and her aunt ate their lunch of rice and chicken by the side of a stream halfway up the Pass. Tsu spread one of the provision boxes with a clean cloth and put their chairs beside it. He had even gathered some branches of flowering wild plum and put them in an empty bottle in the middle of the improvised table, and it was astonishing how quickly he prepared a meal over the hand-sized fire in the cooking tile.

While the ladies ate, the bearers brought out their chopsticks and, filling their plates with food, retired in groups of two or three up and down the rock-walled stream. Suddenly the most distant of these groups burst into an excited chattering, which instantly brought all the others to their side, and even Tsu hurried off to them, slipping on the stones in his fine American shoes.

"What can be the excitement?" Janet asked as the babble increased with the increase of babblers.

"Tsu will soon be back to tell us," Aunt Ione replied calmly, going on with her eating. "With Koreans it can be anything or nothing."

In a few minutes, Tsu, slipping and scrunching, returned and began to give in Korean voluble explanations, to which

Aunt Ione listened, nodding, and then she turned to Janet.

"They've found tiger tracks in the sand by a pool. Tsu says that they aren't fresh. He thinks that the tiger came to drink there, perhaps last evening, possibly at dawn."

"Tiger tracks! Are there really *tigers* here?" Janet's first feeling was one of surprise, but a shiver of uneasiness followed upon it almost immediately. She had heard many stories of tigers carrying people away, even from the heart of villages, or from the midst of a group of travelers. But such tigers had been in India, not here where she and Aunt Ione were eating their luncheon!

Aunt Ione went on with her meal.

"We'll look at them after dessert, if you'd like to," she suggested. "Yes, there are tigers here in the Diamond Mountains. The legend is that they came here with the Buddhist missionaries in 5 A.D. when the monasteries were founded. I believe that this is the only place where they are found north of India."

Janet looked at her aunt, who appeared as calm as ever.

"But Aunt Ione, do you *like* having tigers here? Isn't it dangerous? We haven't a single weapon of any kind."

Mrs. Pattison seemed to consider this for a moment, then turned her bright blue gaze on Janet.

"I never was anywhere where there wasn't danger of some sort. Tarantulas or snakes or tigers or typhoons or falling on the ice or getting drowned while fishing. Just as many people die in Thomaston as anywhere else. I suppose tigers would be called dangerous, but at this time of the year they oughtn't to be very hungry. It's in the winter that they come into the villages for the cattle. I don't think we'll be troubled."

Aunt Ione was so matter-of-fact that Janet laughed and

said ruefully, "I'm not thinking about being troubled, but about being *eaten*."

"Oh, as for that, I've been in the Diamond Mountains four times—this is the fifth—and I'm still here."

After preserved fruit and coffee, Tsu brought fingerbowls filled with cold clear water from the stream, and the two ladies made their way up the channel towards where a remnant of their men were still sitting about on boulders, regarding something in the sand at their feet. Janet was relieved to notice that the Ancients, as she and Aunt Ione called them, were laughing as they ate and talked, yet she had the impression that there was a certain nervousness in their laughter, as there had been in hers.

When she saw the three marks of the tiger's pads in the little pocket of sand among the rocks, she could scarcely believe her eyes.

"But they're *enormous!*" she cried.

"Tracks in mud or sand always look larger than they are," Aunt Ione said comfortably. She spoke for a little while with one of the men, who seemed to know more than the others.

"He thinks that it was a solitary male," she explained. "The cubs usually follow close behind the mother. They say that the males range long distances in a night and that if this is a male he is probably miles away from here by now."

"But a female would perhaps be near with her cub?"

"Possibly." Aunt Ione was casual. Leaving the great pad prints she began to wander alone further up the stream, and Janet rather uneasily followed her. She was glad to see that Tsu had joined them as a bodyguard.

"Are you looking for more tracks?" the girl asked at last. "Don't you think we'd better go back now?"

Just at that moment her aunt gave an exclamation of pleasure and, pausing, motioned Janet to her side. In a cranny between stones, a plant with a flower very like a black trillium was growing. Its three petals seemed to have been cut from dark velvet, and the effect was amusingly artificial.

"We won't pick it," said Aunt Ione. "I just wanted to see one again," and as though satisfied, she turned downstream.

Janet was glad that Tsu was walking behind her. Her back felt very vulnerable.

"I wish the bearers weren't all so old," she remarked after awhile.

Her aunt, walking ahead, turned.

"What did you say, Janet?"

"I wish the bearers weren't all so old."

Mrs. Pattison laughed.

"I chose old ones on purpose. They're all steady family men except Tsu and he has worked for friends of mine and is very highly recommended. The young ones are apt to get drunk and then we'd be in for any amount of trouble."

"But our men would be no good if we *should* meet a tiger."

"Don't worry about that. Young ones would be no better. If a tiger really wants anything, he's apt to get it. It's just a chance like having a rock fall on the trail."

"My goodness, do rocks fall on the trail, too?"

"Not often. I'm afraid I'm a Job's comforter, dear. But when you're in the Orient, you have to take things like tigers in your stride. You'll soon get used to the idea."

By the time they reached the spot where they had lunched, everything had been packed and the chairs were ready for travel. Someone had fastened the sprays of fruit blossom to the carrying poles and their fragrance rose to Janet's nostrils as she arranged herself in her chair.

"Don't you want me to go first?" she called to Aunt Ione, who called back,

"Bless you, child. Forget about that tiger!"

Janet noticed however that none of the jiggy-men wanted to be last in the procession and there was some scuffling and giggling, before the smallest and cleanest of them, the little man who was said to be a Christian, was pushed to the rear.

"You mean old things," Janet exclaimed, aware that she could not be understood. "And you've given him the heaviest load, too."

But her aunt had said that things would go better if they interfered as little as possible with the men, so Janet merely picked out with her eye the biggest and bossiest of the carriers and remarked, "If a tiger gets anyone, I hope it's *you*," and the men, hearing her making the strange sounds which they knew must be a language, laughed aloud at the novelty of her speech, and, refreshed by food and rest, and titillated by the nearness of possible danger, set off merrily, making playful passes at one another with the long staves in their hands.

Within an hour, they had reached the top of the pass. By four o'clock, they had come to a mean, huddled village in a valley surrounded by a solid wall of magnificent peaks. Here, there were plowed fields and low houses half hidden under old thatch, and the children hurried out to see the strangers, shyly smiling. Janet wanted to wipe all their noses but could do nothing but wave and smile at them. Beyond the village on higher land, she could see the long gray-roofed monastery buildings where they were to stay.

As the path began to rise, they passed a field where two men were working in a deep pit and the bearers stopped to exchange talk with them. Something high-pitched in their laughter reminded the girl of tigers.

"What is that pit, Aunt Ione?"

And Aunt Ione answered in her usual tone, "It's a tiger pit. They're repairing the ones around the village. They make them too deep for a tiger to jump out once it's in, and cover them with light brush, hoping that a tiger will really walk on it. I believe one sometimes does."

She must have signaled her bearers, for, still talking volubly with the villagers, they moved on.

Janet called above the chatter, "Have tigers been around recently?"

And her aunt called back, "I believe so."

Janet looked anxiously towards the monastery on the rise above them. It was not one building but a harmonious group, weatherbeaten and noble in proportion, and the fine roofs ended in the upward rise of the eaves, which gave an air of lightness, almost of flying, to the heavy gray tiles. Some of the walls were adorned with faded religious paintings in deep reds and greens, but what seemed important to Janet was that the living quarters opened from a narrow gallery by means of sliding doors of waxed paper.

"What," thought Janet, "is waxed paper to a tiger?" and she was still thinking in such terms when she saw the tall figure of an old man in a square, close-fitting cap and wearing a long gray robe, coming to meet them, followed by two shorter figures also in gray.

Aunt Ione's chair had stopped and she was stepping to the ground. "Come," she called to Janet, "It's the Abbot himself!" and she hurried eagerly forward, while Janet followed a little more slowly, still uneasy and haunted by thoughts of tigers.

[113]

CHAPTER XIII

The Sound in the Night

SITTING with the monks on the gallery in front of the room which had been assigned to them, drinking the honey wine and nibbling on the sweet powdery cakes brought by one of the acolytes, Janet watched the Abbot's face as he talked with Aunt Ione. Those spare lines, that large firm mouth set so kindlily, the eyes deep in the wrinkles of old age and meditation seemed to belong to no one race nor time. It was the face of the ascetic, of the mystic, perhaps even of the saint. Yet if the Abbot's thoughts often dwelt among the great tides of the universe, they quietly and gently came back to the shores of time to welcome his guests.

Janet looked at the other monks. One was short and plump, with a chipmunk's small inquisitive eyes, and the other was a little younger, a stolid sort of man, perhaps rather stupid. Their spirits did not walk with the Abbot's, very far, at least.

In a few minutes, Aunt Ione turned to her niece, bringing her into the conversation.

"The Abbot says that there is to be a pilgrimage tomorrow, and he is particularly glad that we have come in time for it. There will be people from all parts of the country. They are very busy here getting ready."

"What is the pilgrimage about?" Janet asked idly, little

guessing how deeply she was to be involved in this gathering.

Her aunt repeated her question and the Abbot explained.

"It's in honor of the Fifty-three Buddhas," Aunt Ione translated. "They were really missionaries from India bringing Buddhism to Korea. They came by the same route we used over Sleeping Dog Pass almost two thousand years ago, and when they reached this valley they climbed into a tree to meditate for the night. The dragon of the river was afraid of their power and by a great effort of magic whisked the tree away, but what was his surprise to find that because of their extreme holiness, the Buddhas continued to sit on their prayer mats where they were, suspended in air."

The Abbot smiled and said something and the younger monk rose.

"The Abbot suggests that you might like to see the Fifty-three Buddhas," Aunt Ione explained. "It's a beautiful time of the day. If you don't mind, I'll stay here. I know the monastery well."

As Janet rose, all the Ancients within sight hurried up to join the expedition. They were none of them Buddhists and pushed and scrambled at Janet's shoulder, eager to ask questions and to see everything. The first small temple to which the monk led them was the temple of the pilgrimage. Here, under a gaily painted roof, rose from the floor the ragged wheel of a birch tree's roots, painted all colors of the rainbow. Among its intricacies, seated or standing on silk mats of as many colors as the roots, appeared the fifty-three little statues of the Buddhas, covered with gold leaf and all of different sizes.

The Ancients tiptoed about, pointing and counting and now and then giggling. But in the next temple, dedicated to the Guardians of Hell, their delight was even more unbounded. Here beyond the gilded figure of the Judge of the Dead, standing with tears upon his face, the walls were painted with scenes from the Ten Hells, where very red and green devils were busy tormenting the damned.

Janet did not care for this temple, but the old men found it so irresistibly amusing and interesting that they all stayed behind examining the last horrible detail, while Janet followed her guide, past the bell house where hung the great bronze bell, to a little chapel standing by itself.

The mountains had covered the sun with their tapering fingers of stone, and the chapel was shadowy and silent as they came into it. On the wall facing the entrance there was a painting of an old benign man in a long robe, seated under a pine tree by a curling mountain stream. He was reading from a scroll, and on a little bamboo table beside him stood a jug of wine. At his feet stretched a tiger, looking out towards the onlooker, its eyes staring and yellow under a frowning brow. It was nearly life-size and its look was so real and so intent that Janet was startled. She had for the time being forgotten about tigers. Wasn't it enough to have them roaming all over the place without painting pictures of them as well?

Yet something about the chapel fascinated the girl. It was cool and damp and quiet. Only some sparrows in the eaves outside the open door were still sleepily busy with their nest building. Janet stood staring at the painting, which seemed to glow in the twilight. The greens were all pale and almost phosphorescent, and the yellow of the tiger's hide and of his watchful eyes seemed to brighten in the shadows. Behind the beast, the tranquil figure of the old man was faint and peaceful under its pine.

Janet did not know how long she stood staring into the

painting, but she was startled when she heard Aunt Ione's voice beside her saying, "That's the Mountain Spirit."

Janet slowly turned away from the animal stare which had held her.

"But why must they have tigers here?"

The old Abbot was standing beside his guests; smilingly, he explained to Aunt Ione and she interpreted to Janet.

"He says that the tigers are the friends of the monasteries. No tiger ever hurts his brothers who wear the gray robe. All the birds and animals know that the monks love them. Even the crows know it, and when the little boys of the monastery plant the fields in the spring, the crows watch, but they never dig up the seed which is to feed the monks."

For a moment, Janet was caught in the spell of peace. For a moment, the love between tigers and monks seemed real and strong, stronger than fear.

Aunt Ione drew the girl's hand into the comfortable crook of her arm.

"It's supper time," she said cheerfully. "That's what I came to tell you. Tsu has everything ready. The big temple can wait until tomorrow."

Janet was glad to come back to the everyday atmosphere of their quarters and to the box-table, with its candles stuck on plates ringed with flowers, which Tsu had set up on the gallery before their door. They ate a substantial meal while a moon climbed up the eastern sky, still faintly lighted by the sun now sunk beyond the ring of peaks.

"Where will the Ancients sleep?" Janet asked, aware of their ghostly figures seated in a circle beyond them in the courtyard, busy with their bowls and chopsticks.

"Oh, the monastery has places for them. It's just like the

[117]

Middle Ages in Europe. The monastery houses all passers-by who come to it, and feeds them, too. Listen! There's the bell calling the monks to prayer. We shall hear it at midnight and dawn and the chanting of the monks."

"I'm glad that someone's awake most of the time," Janet laughed ruefully.

Yet when she went to bed, she fell asleep almost immediately.

The next day, Janet woke early and lay looking about her, wondering for a little while where she was. A great peony screen across one wall dominated the clean square room, and through the partly open paper doorway, she could see the sunlight beyond their gallery and catch the discreet sound of Tsu's footfalls as he set the table for breakfast.

After the bewilderment of waking, everything seemed familiar and natural. She lay for a little while, thinking about Alan and her family at home and her friends. To her surprise, she wondered what Alex Hunt was doing. She had received half a dozen letters from him, friendly, telling little of himself but a good deal about what was happening to their friends in Thomaston. He always wrote of some meeting with Alan and of what Alan had said, but never mentioned Flo, as the others did. He did not seem to think it necessary to warn her and she was glad of that. Susan Mann was having an affair with Dick Fuller. Janet was not quite sure that they would be happy together and, wondering about happiness, her mind swung to Lydia and stopped, uneasy. Lydia's revelations at the Parker House had been a great shock to her. She had always supposed that if two young people loved each other and got married, they would of course be happy. But Lydia and Jo weren't, or at least, they hadn't been. Why? And were they now?

Janet heard her aunt stir, and returned to Korea and the present.

When breakfast was over, the ladies sat on the gallery and watched the preparations all about them. By late morning, the first pilgrims were arriving, mostly peasants from the villages inland beyond the mountains, their sandals frayed by the hard roads they had traveled, but their faces alight with satisfaction at having arrived at their destination. The Temple of the Fifty-three Buddhas was blue with the incense rising from the joss sticks, and the air carried their fragrance even across the open courtyard. As the pilgrims finished their devotions, they wandered about, sight-seeing among the other temples and chapels, and the two ladies were among the greatest attractions of the monastery. Groups of village women, who had never before seen a white woman, would gather about them, laughing and giggling, touching their shoes and clothes with toil-worn, questioning fingers, whispering to one another and shyly asking the strangers whether or not they were married and how many children they had.

That night, the Abbot and the chief monk, the round-faced man who kept all the accounts of the monastery, dined with Aunt Ione and Janet. As their guests could eat no animal food but loved sweets (of which they had little in their daily diet) the dinner had been planned particularly for them. The main course consisted of mashed potatoes, canned peas and onions to be eaten with a large spoon, since chopsticks were not feasible and forks unaccustomed. Large cups of hot chocolate scented the evening air beside each plate, and a pitcher of condensed milk for the use of the ladies stood in the center of the table beside a larger one of maple syrup intended for the pancakes which they were to have for dessert.

These pitchers caused several small contretemps. While the Abbot was gazing out towards the mountain peaks beyond the roofs, the other monk followed the ladies' example by pouring condensed milk into his chocolate. Having tasted it, he liked it so well that he nearly emptied the rest of the pitcher into his cup.

Tsu, much amused, interfered to tell him that this strange-looking, sweet, white substance was, nevertheless, milk and animal food, and the monk was about to pour the offending chocolate into the courtyard when the Abbot, drawn from his contemplation, stopped him with a gesture and a kindly word.

Aunt Ione interpreted for Janet.

"He says that the lord Buddha is far too great to be disturbed by a small infringement of the regulations begun in error."

The Abbot himself, however, refused the milk, but instead, after a question to Aunt Ione, poured the maple syrup over his potatoes, peas and onions and, stirring them all together, began to eat with evident enjoyment. His companion did the same and Aunt Ione instantly followed suit, as did Janet, who would have made far greater sacrifices than that for the Abbot. Everyone had a second helping of the awful mess, and then Tsu refilled the maple syrup pitcher and began to make pancakes, while the Abbot returned to a gentle contemplation of the peaks, which were so pointed that at such a distance, it was almost impossible to tell stone from pines.

"They are called the Praying Hands," the old man said, returning to this world and a heaping dish of pancakes. "I have lived in this place for more than sixty years and you would think that I would not notice them now. But I never look up at them without a feeling of joy."

The monks did not stay long after the meal was finished, but having made their farewells, returned to take their part in the evening services of the pilgrims.

"At midnight, the torches will be extinguished and the doors of the shrines locked," said the younger man. "Many of the pilgrims will start for home, since there is a full moon. You will find few of them here in the morning."

About half-past ten or eleven, Janet and her aunt, after watching some of the ceremonies, returned to their room and were soon in bed and asleep. The girl's sleep was dreamless; yet suddenly she found herself awake. She had heard something, a terrifying sound, the far-off roar of a tiger, and it seemed to her that she had also heard a scream. The sounds had apparently come from above her in the air. Possibly she had been dreaming after all, for as she sat up in her cot shivering, she could hear no sound at all. The moon-washed courtyard was empty, the monks asleep and silent; not even a night bird gave its cry.

"I haven't thought of tigers all day," Janet scolded herself, "yet here I go imagining nonsense. I couldn't have heard anything or Aunt Ione would have been wakened, too."

And Janet turned on her pillow, determined to put the memory of the hideous sounds out of her mind. But for a long time she lay awake, and only when the white moonlight brightened to dawn did she at last fall asleep.

CHAPTER XIV

The Seventeen Buddhas

JANET WAS awakened next morning by the noise of feet running through the courtyard. Usually the monks, and even the pilgrims, moved almost without sound, their sandals whispering along the paving stones, but there was fear, or some great excitement in this hurry.

Opening her eyes, Janet saw Aunt Ione in her dressing gown standing by their door looking out, her hair hanging over her shoulders in two braids like a girl's.

Seeing that her niece was awake, she said in a low voice, "We'd better get dressed. Something has happened. Those were monks who went by."

Janet jumped up and, putting on her dressing gown, joined her aunt. People were hurrying rather aimlessly to and fro, some running into one chapel, some into another and all talking excitedly. She caught a glimpse of some of the Ancients in the crowd, their long beards wagging. And Tsu was there, hurrying with the others.

"Could it be fire?" Janet asked as she began to dress, and Aunt Ione, already brushing out her hair, shook her head.

"They would be summoning help with the bell."

Just then a deep bronzen cry from the bell on the slope above them broke out, sounding an alarum. It was as though the monastery had found its voice and were calling for aid from the cloudy sky, from the mountains half hidden by drifting mist, from the village below them.

On and on the bell sounded, as the bell ringer smote its bronze side with the swinging padded beam. It throbbed like a huge gong, but just as the vibrations began to lessen, a new blow scattered them with a new deep-throated cry from the bell, which went maddeningly on and on.

The ladies hurried out on the gallery. Looking about them they could see no smoke rolling up from any of the roofs and there seemed to be no crackle of flames. The crowd was thickest in front of the shrine of the Fifty-three Buddhas and as they went towards it, they saw that two monks were guarding the door and allowing no one to enter.

Tsu appeared at their side, his black eyes snapping with excitement. He had the ruddy northern cheeks, ruddier than ever this morning, and he was smiling as he talked.

"A very terrible thing has happened. Last night at midnight after the service the doors of all the shrines were locked. The locks this morning were still in place but seventeen of the Fifty-three Buddhas have been stolen during the night."

The little Christian jiggy-man now joined them.

"It is a miracle," he explained. "God can perform miracles. He wishes to open the people's eyes to the wickedness of idols."

Tsu smiled tolerantly.

"I think it was that old dragon who made the tree disappear when the Buddhas were sitting in its branches. He has been biding his time and gathering his magic and now he has taken some of the Buddhas. Tonight perhaps he will return for another mouthful."

The little jiggy-man became quite excited.

"That is all nonsense!" he shouted, pushing his small innocent face close to Tsu's. "A dragon has no power. The Archangel Michael defeated the Lord of the Dragons and imprisoned him in a palace under the mountains. It is not any dragon who could do such an act." And he spat to show his contempt of dragons.

"I knew a dragon once," began Tsu, enchanted by the argument. Not being a Buddhist himself, his interest in the loss of the Buddhas was impersonal.

But Aunt Ione was deeply troubled.

"Where is the Abbot?" she interrupted.

"He is with the superintendent of the monastery. They are sending out messengers down the valley over Sleeping Dog Pass to question the pilgrims. But in my mind it is as useless as to ask a flock of crows where the grain went to."

Just then there was a further bustle at the end of the courtyard, and the head man of the village appeared with most of the other villagers crowding behind him. They had come fast upon hearing the tolling of the bell, and the older men were panting while the sweat streaked their faces.

A monk ran to meet them and led the head man and the village elders away for a conference with the Abbot.

Later, Aunt Ione had a chance to talk to one of the Abbot's secretaries.

"They have been questioning the young monks who were in charge of fastening the doors," he told her. "They have admitted their wicked carelessness. They locked the shrine of the Fifty-three Buddhas first of all, but without searching it, as they should have done. Then, when all the other doors had been locked, they returned, as is the custom at the time of pilgrimage, for a second visit to make sure that all joss sticks were extinguished and that everything was well. It is

[124]

a rule that one monk shall stand at the door while the other searches the building, but the young men have confessed that they were sleepy and forgetful of their orders. Together they opened the door and walked about the altar and looked into the corners of the room. They have admitted that they were talking together."

While the man spoke, Aunt Ione explained quickly to Janet what he was saying.

"That means that if the thieves were hidden in the building, behind the roots perhaps, they could have slipped out of the open door while the priests were making the rounds?" Janet asked. Aunt Ione nodded.

At first Janet had only thought of the excitement. The whole thing had seemed like a play on a stage. But when Aunt Ione spoke of the Abbot, she felt how heavily this must rest upon his heart.

"What can we do?" she asked anxiously.

"We had better have our breakfast. The more people act as usual, the better it will be. Tsu!" Aunt Ione called a little sharply, in Korean. "We will eat our breakfast as soon as it is ready, and you," she added to the little Christian, "go to the others and tell them that I want them to go about their business. Let them mend their sandals. The young lady and and I expect to visit the Upper Monastery today."

Janet looked at her aunt in astonishment.

"I don't feel a bit like sight-seeing," she objected.

"Neither do I," Aunt Ione agreed. "But at least we can take ourselves and the men out of the way. The Abbot has trouble enough on his hands without having a lot of guests milling about."

By the time they got away, the mist of the earlier morning had cleared; the air was cool and the rising trail beautiful.

To one side of them, a waterfall fell into the valley and Janet could make out steps cut in the rock beside it and a chain to which a climber might hold as he mounted.

As they ascended, the valley narrowed, and before long the path began to climb in earnest. Once they passed between two great boulders with a ten-foot bas-relief of a standing Buddha carved upon each. Once they saw a cave far above them that must have been a chapel, but the steps to it had been broken away and now only the swallows passed in and out at its carved entrance.

They had their lunch in a little meadow strewn with wild flowers and in the early afternoon came to a second valley, smaller than the one which they had left, with a smaller village in it, and a smaller monastery where a smaller Abbot came out to meet them and a smaller acolyte brought them honey wine and bean cakes.

The Ancients, who had at first been rather sulky at being taken away from the excitement at the Lower Monastery, were by this time in their usual high spirits and followed the guide and their ladies about the monastery buildings, showing the greatest interest in all they saw. One or two of them even brought out small soiled notebooks from the breasts of their garments and copied down some of the poems, which had been left by earlier visitors written on strips of paper dangling from the eaves along the front of the main building.

"Looking upon the mountains, I envy the mist which can be always near them," someone had written.

"The autumn leaves do not fall until they hear the temple bells ringing in the twilight," said another; and another ran, "Here the winds of the world are at last still."

Aunt Ione and the little Abbot were old friends, although the Pattisons had never stayed at the Upper Monastery for more than a night or two at a time. He was greatly disturbed by the sacrilege to the Lower Temple.

' A few of the pilgrims spent the night here, but most of them had gone on before the news reached us," he told her. "Of course the rest were questioned. Some of our monks went with the others to overtake the main band of visitors, but I fear they will learn little."

"If the statues aren't found, couldn't more be made?" Janet asked.

The Abbot looked surprised by the question.

"What good would that do? These others are very old. They were made nearly two thousand years ago. In those days, most of Korea had just become Buddhist, not as it is now when the words of the Master are forgotten by all but a very few of us here in the folds of the mountains. The Emperor and the Empress and the Court were all Buddhists then. And when the Empress heard that a temple was to be built, she took the jade and pearl ornaments from her hair and gave them to be sealed into one of the statues, and each of the ladies of the Court gave her ornaments, too. You know it is our belief that just as a person's spirit must be more beautiful than his outward appearance if he is to be admired, so every Buddha must have a treasure within him more precious than the visible gold-leaf outside."

"Is it for the jewels that the thieves have taken the Buddhas?" Janet asked. "Not for the statues themselves?"

"No. Doubtless it is for the jewels. The statues would be too easily recognized, but no living person has ever seen the treasure."

"'Perhaps," suggested Aunt Ione, "if no one knew their history, the ornaments might not seem so unusual."

But the Abbot did not think so. In the old days, the jade

[127]

and pearls and the work in gold and enamel were far more beautiful than anything of today.

"Their loss, I fear, will kill the Abbot," the other Abbot went on. "He will feel, as I should, that there must have been some fault in himself, though he is the best man I have ever known. But Heaven does not judge as men judge."

The ladies were silent on the journey back to the Lower Monastery. It was dark before they reached its shelter and the fireflies were dancing over the field with their bright impersonal gaiety. The moon was late in rising and it was difficult for the bearers to be sure of their footing, so Aunt Ione and Janet walked in single file, preceded by Tsu and followed by the others. The same silent mood seemed to have seized upon them all. No one spoke as they walked ghostlike between the fields, and when at last they reached the monastery, the same heavy silence rested upon its massive buildings and deserted courts. After a quiet supper, the ladies went to bed.

CHAPTER XV

The Valley

Slowly, after the awful rent of the robbery, the fabric of life at the monastery was mended as best it could be and took on its outward routine. But the inner spirit did not return. Gone was the peace in the faces of the monks and the slow tranquility of their walk, the sonorous joy of their chanting. The old Abbot was seldom to be seen in the courtyards, but spent most of the days and nights prostrated before the great image of the Buddha.

"He does not eat," the head monk told Aunt Ione. "If the Buddhas are not found, he will surely die."

On the fourth day, Janet and her aunt met the Abbot as he was coming from questioning a man, who had been brought back to the monastery on suspicion. The stranger had been seen hiding behind some boulders beyond the Upper Monastery and when run down and questioned could not, or would not, give proper answers. The ladies had a glimpse of a big loutish creature, with heavy eyebrows growing in a straight bar across his face, being dragged along, grunting and struggling, between two young monks. The Abbot had risen from his prayers to question him, and, as he was returning to the chapel, Aunt Ione intercepted him.

There was nothing to be learned from the man, he told her

courteously. He was one of those lacking his wits. He had been freed.

Aunt Ione said, "We are grieved for your grief and for the monastery. Would it not be better if my niece and I went to the Upper Monastery?"

The Abbot's weary face lighted up with its old look of kindness.

"I beg you not to go. I feel that help somehow is to come from one of you. It will be a great comfort to me if you will stay."

"Of course we will stay," Aunt Ione said promptly and with a slight bow stood aside while the old man, upright as ever but walking a little feebly and stiffly after his long fast, passed by on his way to the altar.

Janet had been watching the meeting from the steps of the gallery and now she went to join her aunt.

"The man we saw was crazy; they've let him go. I asked if we hadn't better leave but he asked us to stay. He has an idea that one of us might be of help. I have lived long enough in the Orient not to laugh at such foretellings of the future, and yet I can't imagine what either of us can do."

Janet listened to her aunt in wonder. It had not occurred to her that they might be of any use. She had a kind of veneration and love for the Abbot, such as she had never felt for anyone before, except perhaps for her father when she was growing up. How could they help him now? How could she, Janet, help him?

That night she lay long awake, thinking about the robbery, going over the details one by one in her mind. She remembered waking up to see Aunt Ione standing by the door and the sound of the running feet outside. There had been terror in the air, and now she remembered that, during the night, something had happened which had been terrifying also. What was it? And suddenly, she remembered the tiger's roar and the far-off scream which had followed it. She had forgotten all about her lonely awakening in the excitement of the robbery.

Now she lay thinking, and her thoughts came to her very clearly. She alone, apparently, had heard the sounds; she felt certain now that they were connected with the robbery. But how? There had been a bright moon that night, and the thieves—for everyone said that there must have been several to carry the weight of the seventeen statues—must have been on their way to hiding. Janet remembered how the Abbot had told them of the friendship between the monks and the tigers. The tigers were the guardians of the monasteries. A tiger, then, had intercepted the vandals. But where? High up somewhere, higher than the roofs of the monastery. And Janet remembered the stone steps and the iron chain beside the waterfall, which plunged into the valley half a mile away.

Sometimes at night, the real things of every day seem unreal, and truths and values one would never accept by daylight appear self-evident. Now in the quiet darkness, Janet accepted the Abbot's belief that either she or Aunt Ione was to bring help to the Monastery and save his reputation and his life. So sure was she that the answer lay in the tiger's roar that she was equally certain that it was she who was to bring back the stolen Buddhas. She shivered with terror; but the strange certainty persisted. Just as the tiger had let a hundred pilgrims pass and had struck only at the thieves, so he would do nothing to hinder her, so long as she was on the Abbot's business. So sure did she feel of this, at least for the time being, that she went to sleep for a few hours, waking a little before

[131]

dawn, to dress quietly in the chill tenseness which comes before sunrise.

As she stepped into the courtyard without waking her aunt, the light of dawn made everything seem strange and impersonal. The buildings were carved from solid blocks, the bushes and trees from jade. A rooster was crowing from the village as Janet started off.

She did not hurry, not wishing to reach the waterfall out of breath. The path was narrow, and grasses, heavy with the night's dew, brushed against her dress and darkened its hem. Something startled her by dashing across the path almost under her feet. A hawk was already astir in the sky, circling above the valley in long easy curves. The early morning sunlight lay full upon him so that he seemed like a bird in another world from the world of mist and dew and faint shadows in which Janet moved. Most of the peaks were also hidden by streamers of mist but there was one, which caught the light as the hawk did and stood up, high and jagged, with the sun on its distant pines and crevices.

Janet walked along in a kind of trance. Even now, she was not afraid. Behind her, she heard the great bell calling the monks to prayer. As though startled by the sound, a small flock of birds flew up from a bush, wheeling and turning together, twittering as they flew. Janet could see the thin pennon of the waterfall ahead; it seemed to beckon her.

The path was very little traveled, so little that once or twice the girl was uncertain where it went. But with the sound of the falls as guide, she always found it again and in a few minutes came to the edge of the cliff.

The waterfall was a beautiful sight, plunging from sunlight into shadow in endless wavering shafts, but Janet did not linger to admire it. For awhile, the path led among a debris of fallen rocks and then began to mount the solid cliff by a series of steep steps, damp and covered with moss where the skirts of spray were often blown by the wind. The steps were very slippery but, as Janet climbed, the rock became drier and by the time she reached that part of the ascent which was like a ladder, there was no more moss and she was astonished to find nothing as difficult as she had imagined. She discovered that she did not hold onto the old chain at one side but rather gripped the steps above her with her hands as she went up, her dress kilted high and her eyes fixed upward. The bell of the monastery was no longer sounding or perhaps she could not hear it above the near voice of the waterfall. Suddenly, like a hand, she felt the early sunlight upon her head and shoulders, and a moment later she had reached the top of the cliff.

Janet stood breathing deeply and looking with widening eyes upon the scene before her. Hollowed out of the mountains, a valley of perhaps a dozen acres lay at her feet. If the peaks were called by the monks the Praying Hands, this little meadow surely lay in some gigantic palm of stone. There was no apparent entrance or exit from it save by the way she had come, for the second waterfall by which the stream entered the valley, had no steps beside it. All this high eyrie lay steeped in dewy sunshine; so still, so beautiful and so silent, save for the chiding of the water, that it seemed to belong to the innocent beginning of the world and Janet might have been the first person ever to stand at its brink.

But there had been others there before her. Beside the upper falls, on the flat cliff, someone had carved the figure of an old man reading from a scroll while a table with a wine jug and cup stood beside him. It was almost exactly like the painting in the monastery except that here the living stream fell at the figure's feet, and an old, old living pine tree leaned above his head, casting its shadows along the rock.

It was the Mountain Spirit, but there was no tiger with him.

Almost unwillingly, Janet brought her eyes back to the things close about her, and began to follow the ghost of a path. Soon she came upon a worn sandal with its thong broken. A little further on, there was a stain darkening a rock. Janet shuddered but kept on.

CHAPTER XVI

The Three Sacks

Aᴛ ᴛʜᴇ foot of the second waterfall beside the cliff of the Mountain Spirit, the rock lay flat and clear of any underbrush. Janet, standing, looking about her, saw without surprise the stub of a burnt-out torch which had been stuck into a crevice of the rock six feet up the cliff, and beneath it, three sacks of heavy cloth. There had been three thieves then. Two sacks were tied at the mouth with cords, but the third had been opened and beside it lay the figure of one of the Fifty-three Buddhas, face downward upon the stone. A sledge hammer and chisel of native construction, the latter with its top padded with cloth, lay helter-skelter on top of the image and the scarred look of the gold leaf and the deep dent in the bronze showed that several blows must have been struck before the alarm had been given and the intent figure bending over its work had leaped to its feet and fled in headlong and useless flight.

It was as Janet had imagined. The thieves had probably come here, planning to break open the Buddhas, and after a few days of lying hidden to escape in the night with their booty condensed to a small compass, easy to carry and to hide.

But they had counted without the guardian of the Mountain Spirit.

A feeling of pity filled Janet for even these men. They had paid a heavy price for their crime. She had no doubt of what she would find if she should search the long grasses and bushes that edged the meadow; but her business lay only with the Buddhas.

She bent down and opened the sacks. There were five figures in each of the closed sacks and six in the open one and the injured statue on the rock. Everything was there.

Janet picked up the fallen figure in her arms. Its gold nose had been flattened and a hand had been bent, but its expression was as contemplative as ever. The mishaps of the world had not roused it from its long meditation.

"You shall be back on your little mat in no time," she promised it.

Still she felt no fear. She was not even thinking of herself, but only of the joy of the Abbot and of the monks. She stood with the little Buddha held in one arm, looking about her at the Mountain Spirit, at the waterfall, at the meadow. Then, unhurriedly, she started down the path towards the lower falls, carrying the injured Buddha with her.

"We'll get down the steps somehow," she thought, half blinded as the sunlight glittered along the gold leaf, which had for so many hundreds of years known only the shadows of its shrine.

Janet found the Abbot at prayer in the main temple. When she touched his shoulder, the old man slowly rose from his prostrate position before the altar. She could see how weak he had become, but she knew that he would not wish her to make any offer of help, so she only waited until he had straightened himself and looked at her, his exhausted face illumined with joy. He did not need to ask her anything; he guessed by her face that she brought good news, and when he saw that she held one of the Buddhas, the old man reached out his hands for it in a beautiful ritual gesture, as though he were all mankind receiving the bounty of Heaven.

Janet left him then and went to find Aunt Ione, who began asking her a dozen anxious questions. She had scarcely begun to answer them when the head monk hurried up, his prayer beads clicking with his speed. The whole monastery was electric with excitement. News seemed to spread in the community without need for words, and now all the monks and the little boys and the jiggy-men were gathering at a respectful distance, held back by Tsu, his mustaches fairly bristling with excitement and importance.

Aunt Ione explained what had happened, briefly, to the head monk, who instantly gave orders to half a dozen of the younger men; they hurried off to get the Buddhas and to find and bury the dead thieves.

"And now for something to eat," Aunt Ione exclaimed to Tsu, who returned to his cooking tile, while the Ancients came nearer and sat down on their heels, all watching and chattering together in low voices, as they lighted their little pipes and listened to Tsu, who interpreted for them while Janet told her aunt all that had happened. It was clear that Janet's success was their success and would be boasted about in half a dozen villages. The little Christian could not remain quiet, but, jumping to his feet, exclaimed: "Was it a Buddhist who found this lost treasure? No, God gave it to a Christian to do! Christians have power to perform all sorts of wonderful things!"

"I thought you said that the loss of the statues was a punishment on idolators," retorted Tsu from his stone. He was very impartial about religions, but dearly loved an argument.

Aunt Ione, however, had no intention of allowing anything of the kind.

"Tsu," she said, "tell the men that they can go now. Anywhere, it doesn't matter. They won't be needed today; and they have heard all there is to hear."

The Ancients obeyed willingly enough, eager to begin their boasting of the courage and wisdom of their young miss. They were in the highest good humor, pushing at one another and scuffling, their faces creased with smiles, their thin beards wagging. Even the Christian so far forgot himself as to push and scuffle with the rest.

The courtyard was empty now, only the head man of the village and one or two of his elders passed hurriedly by, having apparently heard some rumor, which they came to confirm. Tsu said, as though he had caught the vibration upon the air: "Good! The old Abbot has eaten a little. He'll be all right. He's fasted often, though never before for as long as this."

CHAPTER XVII

The Arrival

CORNELIUS SPRAGUE was not a young man to leave important matters to chance. He was careful of details and to this he attributed a large part of his success in the world. Now as he rode into the village belonging to the Lower Monastery, on a fine morning early in July, he was impatient to be at the end of his journey; he was eager to see Janet, and he was anxious to have a certain question between them settled. He had not intended to bring it up until an entire year had gone by, but the news which had reached him when the *Phoenix* was in Shanghai had determined him, after some consideration, to act sooner.

Yet although it must be considered as a question, Cornelius had very few doubts as to the answer. He was smiling as he rode along on his small sturdy Mongolian pony, flicking at the branches beside the path with the thong of his riding crop and from time to time breaking into a whistle, charmingly gay and birdlike.

He had planned to arrive at the village early, and in spite of the heat and the steepness of the trail he *had* arrived early, as he saw when he drew out the expensive watch from his watch pocket and looked at its dial. The pony was breathing hard but it would get over that, and, if his Chinese servant and the interpreter who followed at the pony's heels were also breathing hard, they, too, would recover.

A different sort of man might have ridden through the village and straight on to the monastery in his eagerness to see the object of his love, but such impetuousness was no part of Cornelius' plan. Although he had ridden mostly above the dust of the trail, his appearance by no means satisfied him.

He turned to the interpreter and said in Chinese: "Tell the owner of the least filthy of these hovels that I will stop with him for an hour while I change my clothes."

Cornelius was soon being bowed into the head man's house. He thanked the old man briefly and ordered him and the women and children to go outside.

His Chinese servant freshened the fire in the stove and heated water for him and while the young man bathed and shaved, the other took out from the saddlebags fresh underclothes, a shirt and a linen suit, which he ironed before presenting to his master.

Cornelius, looking at his image in the small traveling mirror, which his man had hung on the wall at exactly the right height—a lesson it had taken him several sharp rebukes to learn—was well satisfied with what he saw. His clothes fitted his excellent figure perfectly; his waving hair was cut to exactly the right length above his broad brow, and he thought that the added ruddiness of the journey brought out the vigorous line of nose and jaw and made his eyes seem a clearer blue.

His mouth—perhaps the best looking feature in his good-looking face—pursed again and he began whistling a chantey. After all, he was going a-wooing, and his love was a sea captain's daughter.

The servant, among his other duties, had found time with

the help of the interpreter to rub down the pony and brush him into some appearance of smartness, but Cornelius, standing in the door of the head man's house, decided against riding. The pony was small for a long-legged man; he had no intention of appearing before Janet in any manner which might have even a touch of the ridiculous about it. Young girls loved to giggle and tease, and while he did not object to a certain amount of frivolity, he did not mean it to be directed towards himself.

Speaking sharply to his servant because the man had not also found time to change his own blue cotton trousers and close-fitting coat, dusty and darkened with sweat, Cornelius decided in any case to go on alone as he thought his solitary appearance would be more effective.

"When you and this other animal have made yourselves decent, pack the bags and come with the horse to the monastery. See that I have the best room available, looking on the north or east for coolness, and have everything ready as I like it. And here," taking out a small coin, "is something for the old man," and Cornelius, feeling in his pocket to make sure that his wallet and a letter were there, walked superbly through the crowd of villagers which had gathered at the door, glancing at no one, yet not unaware of the tribute of admiration which marked his going.

Cornelius walked slowly. It was nearly four o'clock, as he had planned. He should arrive with the coolness of afternoon and the softening light and other pleasant impressions, but he was in no hurry. He wished to look cool and at ease, as though he had stepped from a magic carpet, had merely appeared, not arrived. Janet would have no warning to give her time to prepare herself for the encounter; but then she was a relatively neat girl and, if she were a little disheveled by the hot day, it would put her at a slight disadvantage, which on the whole might be useful. He had found that to be handsomer and more soigné than his opponent was often a help in a business deal, and what was love but a deal of unusual importance?

As he approached nearer the monastery, appraising its buildings with their ancient paintings on the walls and tilted eaves of gray tile, he saw a girl come out of the temple door and stand looking down the valley as though in uncertainty. Even at that distance he knew her, recognized the resilient slimness of her body and the red-gold light on her hair.

He raised his hand, and instantly her own raised hand answered, and he saw her run down the steps and start towards him. His own heartbeat quickened and his step with it, but he quickly checked himself and returned to his unhurried pace. Let Janet go as fast as she liked. She was coming downhill and not up. Besides, she could afford to be careless. She was being sought and need not be as much on guard as one who was seeking.

Janet did arrive, rosy and out of breath, her hair curly and a little damp with heat, and her face alight with pleasure at seeing him. He almost ventured to kiss her but remembered that he must feel his way carefully.

She was browner and thinner. Her eyes were finer than he remembered. In fact, they were so beautiful that they troubled him a little. He had understood their old rebelliousness and their unshed tears better than the tranquil light in them now.

"Something has happened to you, young lady," he thought, not certain whether this change augured well or ill for him. Like a duelist, he was on his guard behind his smile and his flattering greetings. For one thing, the frankness of her pleasure in seeing him again a little disconcerted him. From his experience with girls in the past, a show of coquetry would have been more promising. But no two cases are alike, and watchful as he was, he enjoyed the walk with Janet back to the monastery. She was eagerly interested in his life in Shanghai.

"How well you are looking!" she exclaimed, and he could see in her eyes that she had forgotten how handsome he was. She enjoyed looking at him, enjoyed his presence there strolling with her up the path, and he spared no effort to be amusing and attentive.

"I can't believe that you're so tall," she said once. "Except for the Abbot, the monks here would scarcely come to your shoulder."

"I hope you like tall men?" he asked but he knew the answer to his question. So he told her about life in Shanghai, about his great house with all its courts.

"The women's apartments have room for four wives, but I should be satisfied with one," he said, with one of his effective short laughs.

"I find my Uncle Theodore very well established," he went on. "The business is even more profitable than I had supposed. And he has overlooked my ineptitude and taken me on as junior partner." His words were carefully modest but there was an assurance behind them, a masculine arrogance, which was not unattractive. "It's about time for me to settle down."

Janet glanced away with a slight blush. She had been so surprised to see a white man walking up the path and, when she recognized Cornelius, she had been so glad to see him, that she had forgotten for the moment to think of herself at

[143]

all. Now she remembered. He had told her that when he saw her again, he would propose—if it still suited his plans—and apparently he was about to do so sooner or later.

Janet reddened with a slight return of self-consciousness.

"How did you know that Aunt Ione and I were here? You must have seen Father in Shanghai. Or did you just happen to come here for a holiday?"

He smiled at her, teasing her gently.

"I do few things by happenstance. No, I knew you were here. Your father told me, and, in fact, I come here as his messenger, to let you know that the *Phoenix* is in port, ready to sail for home. And I have a letter for you."

They had reached the courtyard and now Janet hurried; he was forced to quicken his step or be left behind. She would not be so impetuous when she was a married woman. Girls were like colts, but they should be broken gently. He had more than once seen a very promising young wife ruined by either too much of the curb or the spur. With him, Janet would be in safe hands.

"Aunt Ione! Aunt Ione!" she was calling, all unconscious of his thoughts, and when Aunt Ione appeared from their room Janet exclaimed delightedly, "Mr. Sprague is here! And the *Phoenix* is in port!"

Aunt Ione welcomed the young man warmly, giving him both her hands.

"And my brother?" she asked quickly. "Is he quite safe—and the others? Hasn't there been some epidemic on the Coast?"

"Everyone's safe," said Cornelius looking down at them both, smiling. "You ladies have nothing to trouble about. The smallpox was bad in Shanghai for a time but it has died down now, and no one on the *Phoenix* caught it."

"Thank God!" exclaimed Aunt Ione, "I have been worried about them."

"But Father said it was early for anything of that sort," Janet said in a low voice.

"Yes, but he did not say that there *was* no epidemic. You were fooled, my dear, but I am too old a China-hand to be put off so easily. I saw that he wanted us to be at our ease about the *Phoenix*, so I said nothing further, but I thought a great deal."

Janet looked at her aunt in surprise. What things, about which she never guessed, went on in other people's heads! Just then the Abbot appeared to welcome Cornelius, who, with barely concealed impatience, went through with the ceremony of drinking the inevitable honey wine and eating pine nut cakes. The old man may have felt the new guest's wish to be alone with the ladies, for he left very soon with a kind understanding smile and a gentle glance at Janet.

"Now that the old skeleton-in-skirts is gone," Cornelius began as the Abbot's figure retreated down the court, but at the look of both ladies he realized instantly that he had made a mistake and covered it with a laugh.

"You see how anxious I am to be with you and have you all to myself!" he exclaimed with a disarming boyishness. "I should resent the presence of the President of the United States. I've been dreaming of this moment for days, for weeks, for months really, but especially since I met Captain Pierce and heard the news from Thomaston."

"Good news?" Janet asked quickly. "Mother hasn't been ill, or the children?"

Cornelius shook his head.

"Your family were all in the best of health when your mother wrote. It has nothing to do with them; but you must

[145]

prepare yourself for something of a shock, Miss Pierce. For me, I must say frankly, the news was good news indeed, but I am sorry to be the bearer of any information which may bring you pain."

Janet gave an involuntary gasp but said steadily enough, "Thank you. If there is a letter, may I have it, please?"

He drew an envelope from his pocket and handed it to her without speaking, and stood while she turned and went into the bedroom. Someone had placed a bowl of flowering yellow roses before the painted screen. She noticed them as she entered and saw how beautiful they were. Then she sat down on her cot, looking at nothing. She did not need to open the letter addressed to her father, which she held in her hand. Already she knew what was in it. Alan was engaged to be married, or was married perhaps already, and to Flo, the brazen overdressed cheap Flo whom she had refused to consider as a rival. But Flo had always been a rival, she and her money. Ever since they had been in the Academy, she had always been after Alan, and he had not been able to hold out against her with Janet away so long and her father so opposed to the marriage. Poor Alan! He had tried to be true, she was sure, but knowing that she loved him he had still chosen Flo.

"Father was right. He had to marry a girl with money. But he loved me, he really loved me," she thought, and she remembered how at her door that night after the spelling bee, he had followed her to kiss her again and had said almost wildly, "I will never love any other girl as I love you now."

He had known then that he was saying good-by; but she had never guessed it, never, never, never. All the rest had been mere anti-climax, letting the old cat die, as the children used to call it when anyone stopped swinging a swing and let it go on for awhile by itself, always more slowly and feebly, until at last it came to a full halt. He had allowed their affair to swing on by itself over these months, but on his side, the life had long been out of it. She had felt the change in his letters but had not admitted it to herself. Now the old cat had died.

She repeated the words to herself bitterly. She did not feel anything at all. She opened the letter and found her mother's words—they were engaged, not married. Flo's father was dead and Flo had inherited everything. She was an heiress. Ugly in body, ugly in spirit, all her life she would hang, grinning, on Alan's arm.

And suddenly, Janet began to cry. Lonely and humiliated, she was as sad for Alan's sake as for her own. What a queer thing life was! Lydia had said that it was like this, Lydia, crying her heart out in an ugly hotel room when everyone thought she was so happy.

CHAPTER XVIII

Second Wooing

For more than an hour, Janet struggled for self-control. Then she washed her face and combed her hair. She would *not* be sorry for herself. Let her be honest now; never admitting it to herself, she had inwardly known for a long time that this would happen. It had happened and at last she must face it.

When she appeared again at the door of the bedroom, pale but composed, Cornelius Sprague left his chair by Aunt Ione's side and went forward to meet her, looking at her intently. These last days at the monastery had brought her a new dignity, and she answered his questioning glance with a quiet smile.

"Miss Janet," he asked gently, "would you be willing to play cicerone and show me the sights of the monastery?"

She nodded, glad to be able to translate some of her stifled emotion into action, and as the pair started across the courtyard, Cornelius became aware that a number of elderly men in clothes far too rumpled for self-respecting servants were following them from temple to temple.

"Who in the deuce are those old derelicts?" he asked.

Janet laughed, almost naturally.

"They're our bearers. Aunt Ione and I call them the

Ancients. They always like to go everywhere that we go."

"Very touching," Cornelius said grimly. "Like Mary's lamb. Do you mind if I send them about their business?"

"They'll be disappointed," Janet began doubtfully, but before she could finish, Cornelius had turned and was shouting to the men in Chinese. They did not understand his words but they caught the tone of his voice and made off, surprised.

"You have a very violent lord," one of them said to Cornelius' interpreter, whom he found helping his servant to unfold new quilts for the young man's bed in a carefully swept room. But the servants defended their master with genuine pride.

"He is a prince among men," the interpreter declared. "There is no one like him. He is a lion, a unicorn, a very dragon."

"Tastes differ. I'm glad I serve the ladies."

When the Chinese valet understood this, he grinned broadly.

"Before long, it will be I, and not you, who'll be waiting on the young lady," he remarked as he turned back to his work.

"That will be a long day," muttered the Ancient and went off, talking to himself discontentedly.

Janet felt sorry for her old men. No one had ever in her presence treated them with anything but respect. They were venerable jesters, endeared to her by having shared all the adventures of the mountains. Yet as she turned, frowning a little, towards Cornelius she was once more disarmed by his boyish laugh.

"I want you all to myself," he said, and unconsciously she was comforted to have someone want her, since Alan did not.

In the shrine of the Mountain Spirit she told him a little

about the tiger which had guarded the monastery, and later showed him the Buddhas on their quilted mats in the many-colored roots of the white birch tree. But he did not listen carefully. He did not understand that she had gone alone into the valley above the waterfall and brought back the little Buddha with the battered face from the very haunt of a Bengal tiger, over rocks stained with recently shed blood. He was too intent on his own plans to give more than a cursory attention to what she was saying.

"Yes!" he exclaimed vaguely. "Wonderful! And now, my dear Miss Janet, to return to ourselves, who are alive and young and much more interesting than all the Buddhas and Buddhists in the world, I must tell you what has been burning my lips to be said for an hour. You are beautiful."

"Alive and young!" Janet had seen no one but monks and old people and her Aunt Ione for a long time. And if she were beautiful, Alan did not think so, or at least, no longer cared. Her beauty meant less than Flo's money to him. It was comforting to be courted in this masterful way. Alan had never courted her, never proposed. In April, their hands had begun to meet, in May it was their lips. They had taken it for granted that they would be married. Now he was engaged to someone else, and no doubt she, too, would marry in time.

She felt an arm go about her waist; but she was not ready for this and stiffened and instantly the arm was gone.

"I thought you stumbled," Cornelius said quickly. "Anyway, couldn't you stumble? There are lots of stones to stumble over." His voice showed no annoyance. His face was very close to hers. Handsome as Alan was, his had been a boy's good looks, not a man's.

At dinner that evening, Cornelius took especial pains to be attentive to Aunt Ione, noticing a lessening of the cordiality with which she had greeted him. She remained friendly enough but she had withdrawn into herself and there was a touch of frost in those bright blue eyes. Cornelius, ordinarily, would not have noticed nor cared, but he was on guard today and knew that a very small obstruction may be enough to trip a man. He allowed no suggestion of anxiety however to appear in his manner, which was at the same time deferential and jubilant.

When he turned towards Janet it was with a tender assurance, yet he was careful to take nothing for granted and not to alarm her.

He told amusing stories of Shanghai, he asked the ladies' advice on furnishing his house, he discussed the arts and literature of China and touched upon the political news from home. No one could be more entertaining than young Mr. Sprague when he wished to be, and Janet hung on his words enchanted.

If Cornelius had hoped that she would show self-consciousness when she met him and had been disappointed by her easy friendliness, he had cause to be satisfied now. No one could have doubted their roles. He sat at the table as the wooer and she was the wooed, smiling at his words, lowering her eyes before the sudden assault of his gaze.

"Things are going well," the young man thought, as he pressed forward towards his conquest. If only Captain Pierce were here instead of Mrs. Pattison. Curse that noncommittal voice of hers!

After dinner, Cornelius suggested that Janet should walk out to see the monastery at sunset time. He had noticed a path leading up a hill to the separate building where the monks went to study the scriptures every day. The place was empty now and suited his purpose.

"I know that the climb would be too much for you, ma'am," he said to Aunt Ione, who smiled coldly. This was Janet's affair and she had no intention of interfering in any way. The girl, much less alert than Cornelius, was not even aware of any change in her aunt's original cordiality. She fetched her cloak and when Cornelius held it for her, she felt for a moment the light touch of his hands on her shoulders.

Janet wished that she might go into her room to sit by herself to let her feelings quiet down so that she might see what they were, but Cornelius gave her no respite. He was taking full advantage of the shock which the letter had given her. While her emotions were in a turmoil, he was directing them towards himself, using all the considerable force of his personality, of his wit, of his charm and experience. She had matured greatly in this last year, but though she had been in love once, she had never before been made love to by a man consciously using every trick of the game. She had never even heard that a heart may be caught on the rebound, and she had no defenses against his attack, except her natural dignity. She was bewildered, charmed, but still torn by sorrow for her old love.

As they climbed the path to the Hall of Study, they overtook the sun, which, seen from the temple, had just sunk behind the mountains; but from the terrace in front of the building, they could look into half the splendid disk, red and visible in the mist. Cornelius saw that Janet was in an uncertain mood and for awhile, he held himself to impersonal matters, talking about shipboard days on the *Phoenix*. He had a good memory and a lively sense of the ridiculous and in time he had Janet at her ease. Seeing this, he returned to making love, trying to sweep her off her feet. His wooing was under a pressure of time. For several reasons, he wished to return to the *Phoenix* as her accepted suitor. Not that he was unsure of himself nor of his success, yet like a wise general, he underestimated nothing, and he preferred to have his answer that night.

Side by side, they sat on the steps of the Hall of Study, with the monastery and its activities at their feet, while the light in the west faded from red to rose and then to an ashy gray, and the stars appeared in scattered galaxies on the darkening sky.

Now when their faces were only two glimmers of light turned towards one another, Cornelius abandoned the subterfuges of his love-making, and wooed Janet with triumphant directness, telling her how much he loved her, how beautiful she was, how charming, how dear to his heart in every way, asking her to marry him, telling her how lonely he had been all winter without her, how he had lain awake thinking of her, how her image was so graven in his heart that he never glanced at any other woman except to think how far she fell below Janet in beauty and sweetness.

And as he poured out his words, his listening ear caught the quickening breath beside him and knew that the girl was moved by what he was saying. With a last "I adore you," he reached out and took her into his arms, kissing her again and again.

But, although for a moment Janet did not resist, almost immediately he felt her stiffen as she had stiffened that afternoon when he had put his arm about her waist, and her hands pushed against him as she drew herself from his arms. He, too, rose to his feet.

[153]

Nothing in his voice showed the fury which swept him as he said, "What's the matter, darling? Have I frightened you?"

"It's not you." Her voice hesitated. "It's myself."

Cornelius, accustomed to success, was swept again by sudden rage, but kept it to himself. Janet was not aware of it consciously, yet perhaps his anger made itself felt to some inner sense, for when he went on, "You love me and I love you. Is there anything more?" she answered with more assurance than she had used before.

"I must wait until morning. So much has happened today. You know I just heard of—of Alan's engagement. I don't know what has happened to me. It's almost as though you'd taken his place. But how can a person change so quickly? It doesn't seem possible."

"It often happens," he pressed her. "You've really been in love with me for months, but you didn't admit it because of this boy-and-girl affair. That was only an introduction to love. This is love itself. Don't you feel it? Let me show you. Kiss me and your heart will take my side."

But still she would not kiss him.

"Tomorrow," she kept repeating, "tomorrow, I can tell. You know I can't make a second mistake. Surely you can be patient until tomorrow morning," and nothing he could say would make her let him take her again in his arms.

There was no real reason why he should not wait. He had a fairly accurate idea that Mrs. Pattison would not interfere, yet he had set his heart on having Janet's answer that evening and he did not relish this continued resistance.

He argued a little longer, restraining his impatience, but she still withstood him.

[154]

"Let's go down now. I'm tired and you must be, too, after your long trip. Tomorrow I'll know."

"Of course, darling," he murmured. His low deep voice trembled with controlled exasperation, but it might easily have been with love.

He left her at the door of her room at the monastery. Not willing to risk another refusal, he whispered as they parted, "I shan't ask you to kiss me good night. If you will kiss me good morning, it will make up for the sleepless unhappy night I shall spend." And he did indeed pass a bad night, but possibly not because of love.

CHAPTER XIX

The Departure

J ANET found her aunt propped comfortably in bed reading a book of poetry. It was the only type of reading she ever carried with her ashore, for she could read a poem twenty times over, while a book of prose could be read only once a year at the most and so was not often worth its weight when every pound had to be considered.

"Did you have a good time?" she asked, laying down her book as Janet entered.

"A lovely time," Janet said. But she was exhausted and went to bed almost immediately, though she was too disturbed to sleep.

"How am I to know if this is love?" she wondered, staring into the darkness. She began to go over the evening, word by word, feeling by feeling, and found everywhere a confused whirling of mingled joy and pain, but no answer. She saw Cornelius; he was handsome, rich, assured, adoring. He offered her everything; she would be mistress of his great house in Shanghai in the winter, and in the summer travel to France and England and Germany, or, when she wished, return to Thomaston with such clothes and jewels as Flo had never dreamed of. Why did she hesitate? He had been very understanding and patient, and had not even asked to kiss her when they said good night. Her father liked and approved of him.

There was nothing which could be said against him, except perhaps that he was a little overbearing with the Ancients. But he was a man. And, of course, he wanted to be alone with her. It was natural that he should be a little impatient at the Abbot's visit. Surely he had always attracted her, even on shipboard. Perhaps he was right when he said that she had loved him for a long time without knowing it.

Alan did not want her; why did she hesitate? She would put on her dressing gown and write a note and send Tsu with it so that Cornelius might read it and fall asleep happy. She half sat up in her cot, but after all she was not ready to write the note quite yet. She began to go over everything she could remember about their meeting. On that walk up to the monastery, there had been no confusion, only a pleasant happiness at seeing a friend. But was there anything further back?

Yes, she had stood at the door of the temple looking down the path towards the valley. She had seen a man coming towards her, a white man and young. At first she had not recognized him. She had thought that he would be someone else, Tom Jordan, perhaps. Then she had seen that he was not in uniform; she had guessed who it was. And as she thought, "why, it's Cornelius Sprague," she had felt a wave of disappointment.

Janet stiffened with surprise. Had she been disappointed? Hadn't she just been surprised—perhaps shy? But no, through all the subsequent emotions, that small clear momentary impression remained.

She had been disappointed.

She tried to beat down the memory, to brush it aside as of no importance. She was unwilling to admit its validity against so much else; but she could not forget that she had not really wished to see Cornelius Sprague.

The next morning was bright and cool, and Cornelius, walking across the courtyard from his room, had very few doubts as to Janet's answer. But this would be the last time he allowed her to ruin a night's sleep by her shilly-shallying. The image of a young girl as a colt again returned to his mind. "They need breaking," he thought, and this morning he did not change the word to training.

But his manner as he greeted the ladies was courteous and self-contained. He saw that Janet, too, had had a bad night's sleep. "This is the way she will look in ten years," he thought to himself. Even so, she was still something of a beauty; and in ten years, there'd be no nonsense about her.

She was so grave that he began to feel uneasy.

"If you will excuse me, ma'am, I should like to ask Janet to walk across the court with me."

Mrs. Pattison bowed without speaking, and Janet, looking a little frightened, stepped down from the shelter of the gallery.

"Mr. Sprague," she began hastily as they walked away, not waiting for him to speak, "I am more sorry than I can say to hurt you when you have honored me by asking me to be your wife, but I find that I must refuse."

He turned towards her, his eyes blazing with irritation, yet mastered himself when he spoke.

"Your aunt has influenced you against me! You loved me last night and you love me now."

He saw the surprise on her face. "Why, Aunt Ione has always liked you! No, that's not it at all. No one could turn me against you. I just know deep inside me that I don't want to marry you."

[158]

He laughed in exasperation.

"Janet, Janet, have some common sense! I offer you everything that a woman could wish—my person is not displeasing —you can certainly love and you *do* love me. What would your father want you to do? Why do you think he let me bring you the letter?"

Janet swayed a little under the onslaught of his words, but her gray-green eyes were steady.

"I'm sorry to hurt you, but I cannot marry you."

He turned on his heel and strode back to where Aunt Ione sat on the gallery.

"This is all your work, madam!" he shouted, his rage getting the better of him at last. "You've turned Janet against me!"

Aunt Ione stood up, and her blue eyes met his with a fury as icy as his was hot.

"I used to like you on the *Phoenix*," she said, "but since then you've become like many young men I've met on the China Coast. You are rude to the old and the weak. You are insolent to anyone of another race. They had a saying for it in Thomaston when I was young: Mr. Sprague, you're getting too big for your breeches!"

Before the steady glare of Aunt Ione's blue eyes, Cornelius' lighter eyes fell. If she had been a man, he would have known what to do. He did not look at Janet, but calling for his servants, walked away, headed towards the village.

"Come, your breakfast will get cold," Aunt Ione called. "I don't believe that young man ever had a disappointment before in his life. Don't worry, Janet. It's not his love for you that's hurting him, but just not getting his own way. I wouldn't care to be anywhere around him today. His pony and the servants are going to catch it."

Janet sat down weakly. What an escape! She had seen Cornelius' face contorted and heard his voice thick and ugly with rage. Her eyes and ears had not guessed; her mind had not fathomed what he would be like when crossed, but the tiny warning had reached her, nevertheless.

"I don't believe I'm hungry," she remarked vaguely.

"Eat just the same," said Aunt Ione.

A few minutes later, Cornelius' Chinese servant hurried past, followed by the interpreter leading the horse, saddled, and carrying filled saddlebags.

"Poor things," Aunt Ione's voice was divided between pity and amusement. "But then they're not married to him. They can leave him if they want to. Tsu, this omelet is especially good. Have you more for Miss Janet? And after breakfast, Janet, we must pack; your father will be expecting us as soon as we can get down to the Coast."

The morning was to be an eventful one, marked by an arrival as well as by a departure. A little later, the Abbot set off for one of his somewhat infrequent visits to the village. It was the first time that he had ventured so far since the theft of the seventeen Buddhas, and Aunt Ione watched him go with some misgivings.

"I'd offer to walk down with him," she said to Janet, "but he would not be pleased. He does things in his own time and season. I suppose it's all right. If he feels tired, he'll get the head man to come back with him; but I wish it weren't so hot."

It *was* a hot morning, but in any event the ladies would have stayed at the monastery as they had their packing to do. Tsu and the Ancients had been given orders to have everything in readiness for an early start the next morning, and now they went about, smoking their little pipes and staring at all the pictures on the walls, hoping to remember them when they should be far away from the monastery and all this would be but a dream.

If Tsu and the Ancients felt a pang at parting, Aunt Ione and Janet felt it far more. In particular, the place would always be to Janet the spot where she had begun to learn self-discipline. She was a little worried about the Abbot and now as she folded her clothes neatly and put them in her valise, she kept glancing out of the doorway for his return but still he lingered.

At last, as she sat with her aunt doing some mending, she saw the old man in the distance and put down her sewing.

"There's a man with him," she said.

"The head man, probably," remarked Aunt Ione from the shadows.

"No, it's a white man."

"What! More visitors?" Her aunt came and stood beside her. "Bless my heart, it looks like Mr. Jordan."

"That's what I thought; but he must have known that Cornelius was coming."

"Oh, well, perhaps he wished to come, too."

"Shall we wait here or go to meet them?" It was not like Janet to be unsure of herself in this way. Only yesterday, she had hurried to meet Cornelius Sprague as naturally as a child, but the last twenty-four hours had shaken her.

CHAPTER XX

Again the Phoenix

TOM JORDAN and the Abbot approached slowly. Someone, probably Tom, had cut a staff for the old man, and as they came along the path both were smiling and nodding to one another and carrying on a conversation in a few patched phrases of pidgeon English. Meanwhile, the young man's eyes from time to time glanced keenly at the monastery buildings, and suddenly he saw the ladies and waved vigorously.

The two women waved back and started down the path. Tom watched them approach, his glance resting for a moment on Mrs. Pattison with affectionate interest. He bowed in greeting and then his gaze settled on Janet.

As they came nearer, he saw her fine eyes fill with concern.

"Why, Mr. Jordan!" she exclaimed, "what has happened to you?"

He grinned rather sheepishly.

"I had a little disagreement with someone this morning. It's nothing. I tried to wash at a stream, but I guess I didn't do a good job."

"You and Mr. Sprague had a fight?" asked Aunt Ione as she shook hands.

"He was in a bad temper about something and tried to

ride me down. I pulled him out of the saddle and we had a little argument, which made us both feel better. We've been itching for it ever since he boarded the *Phoenix* at Shanghai."

"Who won?" Aunt Ione persisted with frank interest, while Janet looked worriedly at the mate's cut mouth and one eye which was nearly closed. There was blood, too, dried on his shirt front and uniform. Never a handsome man, his pleasant freckled face had not been improved by the battle, but there was a twinkle deep back in the open eye and the mouth, swollen as it was, smiled as he answered.

"It was nearly a tie. He's no handsomer than I am at this moment. Now we'll get the old gentleman home and I'll tell you all the news."

Tom had, as they guessed, met the Abbot sitting exhausted by the side of the path on his way back to the monastery and had taken steps to convoy him home to safety.

Now, when the old man had gone to his own quarters, Tom said eagerly, "Did Sprague tell you my news? No, of course, he wouldn't. Well, the company has given me the *Falcon* when she's off the ways. I'm to be her first captain. Captain Pierce was kind enough to recommend me." He looked at Janet eagerly, and she reached out and shook hands.

"Captain Jordan, let me congratulate you!"

"You're the first to say that—I mean to call me Captain Jordan—Miss Pierce. I'm sure to be lucky after this."

Aunt Ione shook hands, too.

"I still want to know how you *both* happened to come?"

"I was to have come, but when Sprague talked to Captain Pierce in Shanghai, the Captain told him that he might bring up the letter from Mrs. Pierce. But I still wanted to come, so after my shore leave began I came along; of course, I didn't get off right away and I couldn't find a horse to hire so I got here late. Did he tell you I was coming? No?"

Aunt Ione laughed her rather whickering laugh.

"Would he be likely to?" she asked. "That young man has nothing on his mind except plans to feather his own nest."

The ladies spent the day going about the monastery for the last time, saying good-by to the places and the people they had learned to love. Tom Jordan accompanied them, and that evening all three dined for a last time with the Abbot and his head monks. It had rained a little in the afternoon but towards evening the sun had forced its way through the clouds, and, while they ate at a table in the courtyard, the red light of sunset shone brightly along the wet pavements and struck the old temples into a strange brilliance, so that they glowed and glistened against the clouds still black behind them. It was a beautiful moment, filled with the sense of transience, and Janet and Aunt Ione felt all the sadness of parting, knowing that even if some day in the future they should return, the Abbot would no longer be there, nor would Janet be young and filled with the sweet painful perplexities of youth. Tom Jordan, aware of their mood, was quiet also, and the monks seemed to share something of the same melancholy.

Only the tall old Abbot was too wise and too old to be sad. His face and talk were joyous, like a young child's, and slowly he won them back to conversation and laughter. At the end of the meal, he sent a little boy for a package wrapped in a square of old brocade and gave it to Janet. When she opened it, she saw an amber carving of a tiger. The creature was lying down, its head raised from its outstretched paws, its eyes staring out under a furrowed brow. The last rays of the sunset struck along the amber until it shone like fire.

[164]

"To remember us by," said the Abbot. "It is very old; part of the treasure of the monastery. My brothers and I think it but a small return to one who has saved the honor of our community."

The beautiful thing lay along Janet's palm, almost without weight and warm to the touch; like nothing of metal, glass or china, nor any jewel. She had seen many wonderful things in the Orient but nothing she could have cared for as she would care for this.

"I shall keep it all my life, grateful that I was able to be of any service," she said with a tender dignity, which Tom Jordan had never seen in her before. "She is changed; she is a woman now," he thought. With him, too, things had changed. At last he was in a position to marry. He was a captain. But he knew that Janet, within the last twenty-four hours, had gone through one emotional crisis in reading the letter, and he suspected that there had been another as well. If he had anything to say to her, any question to put, this was not the time.

They left early the next morning and the Abbot and all the monks accompanied them for a little way on their journey. As they passed through the village, everyone came out of the houses to bid them farewell. Then their straggling caravan was once more alone, winding through the mountains, along the edge of the stream in whose sands Janet had first seen the mark of a tiger's pads. The trees were in full leaf now; there were few flowers, and the birds were no longer singing in the ravine. As the path grew steeper, Janet left her chair to scramble downhill with Tom Jordan, and Aunt Ione sometimes joined them to rest her carriers. The jiggy-men had light loads now; there were few supplies left in their boxes. Tsu's pots and pans rattled as their bearers ran, and Tsu himself had stuck a wild rose behind the visor of the American cap of which he was so proud.

They were going down out of the mountains, out of the secret valleys, out of the enchanted world of monks and tigers. Before them stretched the flat, far-off rice fields and the sea, which seemed to rise up like a vast blue cup, until its rim stood against the sky as high as the mountainside down which they were hurrying. Far-off and very small, they could see the *Phoenix,* like an anchored toy smaller than a matchbox, a mere dot of something in the harbor. And they could make out the inn where they had spent the night on the way up. But now they were traveling so fast that they would reach the shore before dark.

The Ancients were going home. They had not been homesick; they had enjoyed the excursion and had relished all the excitement of the theft of the Buddhas, but now that their faces were turned towards the east, now that they saw the sea before them, they were filled with a wild gaiety. They cackled and ran races, their skinny old legs seemed tireless, and burdened as they still were, it was all that Tom Jordan and Janet could do to keep up with them, and Aunt Ione panted and laughed and after awhile summoned her bearers to stop so that she might be carried again for a little way. But Janet would not return to her chair. The excitement of the Ancients she shared in her own heart.

There lay the *Phoenix,* and she, too, was going home. From now on, their faces were set towards Thomaston, though they must sail almost to the South Pole to reach it. Alan was no longer waiting for her. Still it was home; the people and the things she had known all her life. She had been long enough in strange ports. She was going home and she hurried on, leaping from rock to rock in the rough trail, laughing and joking with Tom Jordan over her shoulder, almost as tireless as the Ancients.

It was hard to take time to stop for luncheon by the stream, but Aunt Ione insisted upon a halt and a rest for everyone, and once their mad career had been broken in upon, they were glad to sit down and eat.

"Yes," said Aunt Ione, "*and* dessert. And not a person starts down the trail for half an hour after the last bite has been taken. Janet, you'll be exhausted tonight."

But Janet was not exhausted. They reached the plain in the early afternoon and then Janet was willing to return to her chair. How the rice had grown since they had been gone! And the frogs were not so much in evidence. It was almost dark before they came to the sea, but Captain Pierce had seen them coming and had rowed ashore to meet them. First he kissed his sister and then Janet. Her arms went about him in the old warm way and as she kissed him, she whispered, "You were right about Alan, Father."

He patted her shoulder. She was his girl, generous-hearted, not afraid to admit when she had been wrong. Well, he could be generous, too, as he would show her.

CHAPTER XXI

Conversation at Sea

THE morning when Aunt Ione and Janet went ashore with the Ancients to return the cots and chairs to Mr. Cockrane, it was raining and all the eaves of the houses dripped with rain and their feet splashed in gray puddles. Yet even after the things had been delivered and the last of the supplies had been distributed among the bearers and their wages paid with a bonus for their good behaviour, neither Tsu nor the old men were willing to leave, but mournfully followed the Americans back to the wharf and waited, like white-clad scarecrows, until the anchor was weighed and the *Phoenix* stood out to sea. They had been so proud of their blue-eyed ladies! And for years, they would talk of how the young miss had gone into the valley of the tiger to bring back the Buddhas. Tsu had suggested returning to America as their servant, to cook their rice and to look after them always, but Aunt Ione had explained how impossible that would be. Yet she and Janet were sad, too, as they stood under their umbrellas and waved good-by to their companions and Korea.

For the first time since they had left home, Janet came down with a cold and retired to her cabin for several days of sneezing and rest. When she emerged, it was to find the decks sunny and her chair waiting beside Aunt Ione's and the warbler still in his cage out of reach of Mattie, who was now the proud mother of three striped kittens with white paws.

"Why, their eyes slant!" Janet exclaimed delightedly. "That comes from being born in China."

There were a dozen ducks in coops, far too pretty to be eaten, Janet thought, and a pair of half-grown pigs of a leaner type than she had ever known, and at Honolulu Captain Pierce bought a cow.

"The passage around the Horn should be much easier with the prevailing winds behind us, if we are in luck. It will be pleasant to have fresh milk."

The milk made a great difference in the taste of the food, and when, later, on the way up the eastern coast of South America, one of the crew came down with a suspicion of scurvy, the milk soon put him on his feet again.

While the *Phoenix* was in Honolulu, the Captain and Aunt Ione and Janet took a carriage and drove out to call on Mr. and Mrs. Sprague, who received them very coolly. As they drove back to the ship, Captain Pierce laughed, "No manners, any of them," he said. "The young man lost little time in sending on the news of your rebuff, Janet. The evening he arrived at the beach, there happened to be a native coasting vessel in the roadstead and he signalled her and went aboard without coming near the *Phoenix*. Mr. Hinks was going ashore and saw him as he was being rowed out, and he told me that he was quite a sight, as though he'd been in a barroom fight. Mr. Hinks hailed young Sprague but got no answer. I don't like to see a man lose with such poor grace! He must have sent a letter off by some vessel the very next day, to have news of your hard heart, Janet, reach here before us."

"Thank goodness I *did* say 'no,'" and Janet gave a shiver. "What cold proud eyes they both have."

It was on that same evening that Captain Pierce drew Janet aside to talk with her as night darkened the sharp edges of the Pali and the first high stars appeared one by one.

"You know, Janet," he said, going straight to the point, "that I favored young Sprague as a suitor. I hoped that you would marry him. He seemed to me likely to succeed in life, to come of a good family, to be himself a fine young fellow and very fond of you. His behavior after you refused him has made me feel very differently about him; to have married him would have been a great mistake. I was wrong in my judgment."

Janet, who was standing beside her father, took his arm and laid her cheek against it, without speaking.

"In fact," Captain Pierce went on, "I was at least as mistaken as you had been. This makes me feel that I had better not pick out a husband for you." He laughed shortly, and was silent for a moment. Then he said, "If you still wish to marry Alan Loring, I withdraw my opposition. I should expect to continue your allowance."

"Father, I can't say how happy your trust makes me," Janet answered in a low voice. "But of course Alan is engaged now to Flo."

"They can't get married until summer, a year after her father's death." Captain Pierce's voice was matter-of-fact. "I should not consider the feelings of that wretched girl for a moment. She had no compunction in taking him away from you. If you claim him now, he was yours orginally."

"But he's chosen her."

"For lack of better. And she was on the spot and always

after him. Alan is not a strong man, my dear, and it takes a strong man to withstand the will of a determined girl."

"And if I were as determined as Flo?"

"You'd get him. You have beauty and brains, and so long as he knows that I have withdrawn my opposition, even her being an heiress would not weigh down the balance in her favor, I'm sure; that is, if you still want him."

"How business-like it all sounds!"

"Its time to see things as they are, not in a rosy mist. Again I say, Alan Loring isn't worth much but there's nothing bad about him, and if you want him, take him and good luck!"

He heard her sigh deeply, but for a long time she did not speak. Then, at last, she said rather sadly,

"Thank you, Father. You have been very generous. Please don't tell anyone, even Mother, about this. I don't know what to say. It isn't always easy to know what is in one's heart, is it?"

He patted her hand.

"There are many other young men," he said cheerfully. "I merely wanted you to know that I shall respect your decision, whatever it may be. You are far more experienced than you were a year ago."

And with that, the conversation broke off and was never renewed again.

The voyage home seemed far quicker than the voyage out, even though it took nearly as long in actual time. They had their share of rough weather, of head winds and calms, but they gained time at the Horn, which they cleared in three days with a tail wind behind them all the way.

Once there was trouble with a new hand who shipped on

[171]

at Shanghai, a Southerner from Georgia. For some reason, Mr. Hinks, the second mate, took a dislike to him and bullied him persistently like a horse-fly. His tyranny was not particularly noticeable but it was unending. Some surly quality in the mate found relief in this constant petty persecution. Once or twice, the Captain spoke to him about it. "Let up on Bates," he advised. "You're after him too much, Mister." And the second mate was more careful when the Captain was on hand, but the infuriating nagging continued, until, one afternoon, when the sailor—driven beside himself—drew a knife and made at the officer.

Another sailor tripped him up and Bates was put in irons and given bread and water for a week. Mr. Hinks demanded that he be kept in irons for the rest of the voyage, declaring that his own life wasn't worth a bent penny once the man was free, but Captain Pierce eyed him coldly.

"You brought this on yourself, Mister," he said. "If there's further trouble, it's you whom I'll put in irons. For the sake of discipline, I punished the man, but I know where the fault lies." And he ordered up Bates; gave him a withering lecture upon his duties aboard ship, changed him over into the first mate's watch, and the ill feeling died down.

On this homeward voyage, Janet learned a great deal about navigation. Tom Jordan taught her, and her father was surprised to find her able to make a dead reckoning and set a course. She would spend hours over her figures and come out with the same answer as the mate's, not altogether to Mr. Hinks' satisfaction.

"By glory, you'd make a good wife for a captain!" her father exclaimed one day. "You could navigate a vessel if he were down with fever."

"I wouldn't be the first Thomaston woman who has," Janet

laughed. "Do you remember Mrs. Jenson and poor Mrs. Molly Davis, when her husband was drowned off Hatteras?"

"Should you like to be a captain's wife?" the mate asked casually.

And Janet laughed again.

"It would depend on the captain. What do you think, Aunt Ione?"

"As you say, it would depend."

Tom Jordan never pressed the question further. Perhaps he sensed Janet's own uncertainties. And then he was not yet a captain, and though Janet was with him constantly and always showed the greatest friendliness, she never made any opening for possible love-making.

The *Phoenix* put in at Rio for fresh food and there were the usual letters from home and one from Lydia announcing, with joyous pride, the birth of a son, John Pierce Loomis.

"Now I'm sure she's happy," Janet thought with relief, for Lydia had been much on her mind, and whenever she remembered her careless mailing of Lydia's letter to Jo, she had felt a sense of guilt as well. Now, surely, everything must be all right, or at least better—or was Lydia still pretending? Perhaps the baby was sickly and Jo couldn't bear the sight of it and Lydia was up night after night with it when it cried and looked like a wreck and was more unhappy than ever? Life wasn't the way young girls dreamed: an adoring husband, a beautiful happy baby who only woke up to smile and eat and go to sleep again, a little house always neat and pretty. What was Lydia's life actually?

But now they were off Florida and it was only November; Captain Pierce said that with luck they should be home by Christmas. Even the sailors, whose homes were often nothing but a rented room up two flights of stairs in some slatternly

[173]

waterfront boarding house, were as eager as Janet to be there by Christmas, whatever that might mean to them. But words have great powers of association, and home and Christmas rang together like a chime of bells all up the coast, past Georgia, past the long banks off the Carolinas, and the Capes of the Delaware. They met a blizzard off Long Island but even that scarcely delayed them, and on December twentieth, they sighted Monomoy and the twin lights of Chatham, and on the twenty-third, picked up the pilot off Boston Light and stood down the harbor on a bright day, with the islands and the Blue Hills white with snow between blue water and blue sky.

The *Phoenix* had been sighted off Cape Cod and all the family were on the wharf to meet her as she came in; even Lydia and the baby, wrapped in a fur robe; even Jo Loomis waving with the rest. And behind Jo, standing a little off from the others as though to say, "I am not one of the family, merely a friend," there was Alex Hunt, looking taller and thinner than Janet remembered as he stood quietly smiling upward at her where she stood by the rail.

CHAPTER XXII

Conversation on a Train

"When I got home that evening," said Lydia, when at last the girls were alone in Janet's room, "Jo was gone and the house was empty. He didn't get back until late that night. He'd been to Boston after me and of course the *Phoenix* had sailed and no one could tell him anything."

"He'd read the letter?"

"Of course he'd read the letter. He was furious. He raged and he stormed at me for hours. Then he forgave me. It was like the old courting days. We could *talk*. You see the trouble had been that I was so much in love with him that I'd never given him a moment's peace. You know, Jo's an only child and used to being a lot by himself, and I drove him nearly crazy."

Lydia spoke with relish.

"So he wanted less attention? I thought husbands usually wanted more."

"Not in our case. Not at first, at least." Lydia looked down at her hands and laughed. "Now that Baby takes up so much of my time, Jo really feels out of it. Jan, he's almost *jealous* of his son! He says he never has me to himself anymore," and Lydia laughed again, and Janet laughed with her. This was a different Lydia, Lydia as she used to be when she was the big sister at home, with her beaux and her parties, sure that the world was full of love.

"You'll find that you have to manage a husband," Lydia went on, turning more serious. "By the way, were you very upset by Alan's engagement to that terrible girl—what's her name, Flo something or other? It must have been an awful surprise, hearing it like that on the other side of the world."

Janet smiled and nodded, but she had no confidences to give on the subject. Perhaps talking with Lydia might have been a good thing, but she herself did not know what to say, for she was not certain what she felt. She turned the subject back to family matters.

"Mother's looking well and the children have grown a foot. But it's Steve who's changed most. I never thought about him as being handsome, but now he's a perfect lady-killer."

"So Mother says. Steve still spends most of his allowance on candy but now he takes it to the girls. He and Millard go calling together and Mother says they're very popular."

"He used to have trouble at school."

"I think he's doing all right. Anyhow, Mother doesn't seem to be worried. Its Deborah's teeth now. They're coming in crooked, she says. Mother is worried about something all the time, I guess."

"Deborah looked all right to me. Very pretty. But maybe I didn't notice when she smiled. There was such a milling around that I didn't *really* see or hear anyone."

"Yes, darling, that's why I left Baby with Mother and insisted upon coming up with you while you unpacked for the night. We can't come home for Christmas this year when Baby's so young, and I did want to have a good talk with you before we had to catch the three o'clock train. I wanted to tell

[176]

you how wonderfully everything has worked out. It was all your doing, sending my letter when you did, though I was furious at the time, of course."

"How funny life is." Janet had taken off her hat and furs and perched now on the bed while Lydia sat in the red upholstered chair with long fringes which stood by the window. "I did a stupid careless thing and it upsets Jo, and breaks down the wall of not being able to talk things out which had grown up between you. Yet it was heedless just the same. And sometimes a person might do something beautiful and thoughtful and good and yet ruin another person's life by it."

"Jan, stop being so serious! You're just home, looking simply divine, and I'm sure that nice young mate's mad about you and here Alexander Hunt has come all the way up to Boston just to see you come in! You're going to have a wonderful time."

"Tom Jordan's just a friend and so's Alex Hunt. He's the most thoughtful boy I've ever known. He knew I'd be feeling badly about Alan and so he came along to show me that the old crowd would be glad to see me. It was dear of him, but it doesn't mean anything the way you mean."

"Don't be too sure. I watched his face when he shook hands with you. And Mr. Jordan's when he said good-by. If they're not in love, I'm a nanny goat."

"Foolish Lydia, you see love everywhere. It's just because you're in love with Jo and he's in love with you."

Lydia jumped to her feet and gave Janet an affectionate hug and kiss.

"I must go find Mother and see if Baby's been a good boy. But I did want to tell you everything! If you get a darling husband like Jo and a wonderful baby, too, you'll probably be as happy as I am."

[177]

She drew back, looking at Janet's face with clear bright eyes.

"And maybe even happier. You're the loveliest looking thing I ever saw. Its lucky you weren't grown up when Jo was courting or he'd never have looked at me."

"Nonsense," said Janet. "Alan prefers Flo."

But Lydia was already at the door.

"Come along; Baby may need me. You know he recognizes me now and smiles; yes, really smiles. By the way, wasn't that young man who got on the *Phoenix* Cornelius Sprague? Thinking about it afterwards, I was sure I had seen him before, but I was too excited to make connections at the time. Jo and I used to see him two or three winters ago; Jo rather liked him but I detested him. He had such an arrogant way of looking at people. But lots of women found him very attractive. What did you think?"

"I ended by thinking as you do."

They were in the corridor now on the way to Mrs. Pierce's room and Lydia gave Janet's arm a pinch.

"What a sly puss you are! You say so little about yourself. Really, you're aggravating!"

But just then they heard a baby begin to cry and Lydia had no thought for anything else.

Soon after, the three Loomises had to go, and an hour later Aunt Ione took the train for Providence, though every effort was made to urge her to come to Thomaston for the holidays.

"I've been a long time away," she said. "I must see that my house is in order and talk to my man-of-business and greet my friends. I'll come on a summer visit."

The good-by between Janet and Aunt Ione was brief but deeply felt.

"Call on me at any time for anything," the older woman

[178]

said, her bright eyes for once a little misty. "If I had had a daughter, I should have wished her to be like you, Janet."

Before Janet could make any answer, Aunt Ione had whipped out a handkerchief, blown her nose briskly, and turned to the others, and in a matter of minutes, she drove away with Captain Pierce, who was seeing her off.

Next morning, the family caught the morning train. "How beautiful," Janet thought, "the snow is!" Even the engine smoke, puffing out in great white garlands, looked beautiful to her and the shapes of the elms and oaks and the thin shadowy thickets and the dark grave green of the pines when they passed a stretch of woodland.

There was smoke drifting from at least one chimney of every house and usually from two or three, and the little children were coasting on the slopes, while their older brothers and sisters fretted at their lessons in school. Along the road the pungs and sleighs went by, and she knew that the sleigh-bells were ringing across the clear air.

What wonderful things she had seen and yet was anything more wonderful than this? She looked at it all with eyes refreshed by absence and noticed details which in the old days she would have taken for granted. Yet, though her eyes were as perceptive as a stranger's might have been, her heart was her own; and all the landscape spoke to her of her childhood and her girlhood and was warmed and endeared by a thousand memories.

Her mother was sitting beside her father, with Deborah and Ted in the seat in front of them where their elders could keep an eye on them. Steve sat for awhile with Janet, a little back in the car, but growing restless after the first hour, he wandered off to see if there were anyone whom he knew on the train. Alex Hunt took his seat.

For a while, the two were rather silent, then Alex said in a low voice, "You're as pretty as ever, Jan."

Janet turned away from the window to look at him in surprise, but before she could speak, he went on.

"You know I'm working at Mr. Beale's. Next year he's retiring and he has made it possible for me to take over the store. I have plans ultimately for enlarging it. And some day I hope to buy blueberry lands in the Cherryfield district. There's a future in blueberries. When I have enough money, I'll run for the legislature and I'd like to start a newspaper."

She had never noticed before what nice hands Alex had, very sure in the few gestures they made. And his quiet voice moved her. What he said came from something deep in him, deep and sure, too. He had always been a good mixer, but his true life was lived when he was by himself—the boys used to call him crazy because he had his own thoughts. Now after being away, she saw him with new eyes, and his face, which she had never before thought handsome, held her by its look of warm kindness and purpose.

Janet did not try to interrupt, but nodded and waited almost with anxiety, for she saw by a whitening of the knuckles of the hand on his knee that what he had to say was something which meant a great deal to him.

"I've thought this all out," he went on at last. "I've been in love with you since we were in grammar school. No, don't say anything. I know you haven't had time to think about me at all. But I wanted you to know. As long as Alan was around I knew I didn't have a chance."

Janet's heart had quickened and then seemed almost to stop as he spoke. She flashed a look upwards at him, surprised, yet not surprised. There had always been a special feeling between them, but it was true that in the old days she had never stopped to think about it. Yet even when she was a little girl, she had gone to Alex for reassurance when she was unhappy about anything, and, on her part, she had always been furious when the children made fun of his outgrown clothes or his interest in things which didn't interest them.

"Do you still write poetry?" she asked, and he laughed suddenly.

"They're getting better. You must see for yourself."

"I'd like to."

He seemed quite satisfied to have her talk of poetry and not of love. He required no answer from her. And yet in a little while she found herself saying, "Alex, I want you to know something, too. I don't feel free even now."

He turned to her sharply.

"What do you mean?"

"It was something Father said that started me thinking—" She paused, unable to go on.

"About Alan?"

"Yes, about Alan."

"But—"

"I know. I was away and Flo was always after him—if he is happy, that's all I want. But suppose he's miserable? When you have loved a person with all your heart, can you just stop loving him overnight, Alex, and never care what happens to him?"

"Jan, you're talking nonsense. You don't owe Alan a thing. You can't tie to good looks if there's nothing back of them. He had his chance—"

"And lost it. I tell myself that, too. But Flo is nothing new. She was always there, only I wouldn't admit it. She stepped forward while I was gone. When I come back—"

"He jilted you," Alex said harshly. "The whole town knows

[181]

it. Jilted you for money. Marry anyone you like, Jan, except Alan Loring."

She did not speak at once and then she said, "Words don't frighten me, Alex. Words like 'jilted' I mean. They did at first, but not any more."

"Its an ugly word for an ugly thing."

Janet sighed and looked out of the window again without answering. The car smelled of plush and cinders and she could hear the steady beat of the wheels on the steel tracks and the engine hooting fiercely as they approached a crossing.

When after awhile they began to talk again, it was about other things. Eighteen months lay between them like a river to be bridged. There were a hundred questions to be asked and answered, and before they knew it the conductor was shouting "Rockland" along the aisle and taking down from the overhead racks the valises belonging to unaccompanied ladies.

Half the town was on the platform to meet Janet, and Alex disapppeared in the surge of welcome that surrounded her. She was kissed and hugged and shaken by the hand until she was dizzy, but, although she talked and laughed and said all the right things, she was really aware of only two people in all that jubilant crowd.

CHAPTER XXIII

Time Turns Back

THE Christmas holidays that winter ushered in a particularly gay season. Never had the snow seemed so white, the air so exhilarating, the stars so clear. There were coasting parties and skating parties and sleigh rides, candy pulls, suppers, dances and charades. Almost every evening, Janet was off, escorted sometimes by one young man and sometimes by another. She had suitors from Warren and Rockland: young Fiske, who had gone into the lumber business with his father, and Captain Isaiah Lincoln, who was a widower at thirty, with one shy little daughter in need of a mother. It was known that she heard from a Captain Jordan who had been mate on the *Phoenix*. Most often she was seen with Alex Hunt, and it was about him that her friends usually teased her. But she only laughed and said nothing. Two years ago, the whole town knew that she was in love with Alan Loring. Now, no one knew anything about how she felt, not even her mother.

"I wish I understood Janet these days," Mrs. Pierce said more than once to Captain Pierce, who was staying home until late April or May, while the *Phoenix* went into drydock. "Since she came back, she's been very different. She used to say everything she thought as soon as it came into her head, and now I can't tell what she's thinking."

"She's growing up, that's all," Captain Pierce would reply. "She has a very important problem to work out. You'll know when she has the answer."

"I suppose so." Mrs. Pierce would look worried and then remark with a clearing brow, "Isn't Stephen improved? Mr. Lorimer says he's near the head of his class at the Academy. And he's always coaxing Minnie to wash and iron extra shirts for him. I thought I'd never live to see the day."

"They're growing up! Even Deborah's quite a lapful, and getting to the saucy stage these days. Before you know it, Adelaide, they'll all be married and off and then what will you do?"

"I'll still have you, and you'll be here at home. When the last one marries, you'll retire, if you haven't done it already; and we'll live contentedly and the children will come to visit us and bring the grandchildren."

"Yes," said the Captain, "I'll be an old man then. I'll be ready to retire and sit by the fire and tell young men how a vessel ought to be sailed."

His wife laughed.

"There are four to marry off first. You have some years ahead, John, before you're beached."

Janet came in just then, her fur hood and cloak smelling of snow and the starry night outside, and her face rosy with the cold. She had been tobogganing at Peck's Hill.

"Such a lovely night!" she said, shaking a loose glisten of snow from her shoulders. "It began to snow an hour ago. All the flakes were as large as quarters and they hung in the air. We could scarcely see where we were going and the toboggans kept upsetting, but it was like being upset among feathers."

"Wouldn't Alex come in?"

"No, he has to go to work at the store early tomorrow. They're taking stock."

Janet was sleepy, too, and went to her room, but once she had closed the door, her gay mood left her. Before she lighted the gas, she went to her window and looked out across the snowy yard to the Loring house next door. Would she never be free to take up her own life? There were lights downstairs and one in the upstairs hallway, but none in Alan's room and she knew that he must be out with Flo. Flo kept him constantly at her side. When she met them at parties it was Flo who talked, not Alan, Flo dressed in half-mourning, hanging on his arm, sending him on errands to get her scarf or muff, looking at Janet with hostile triumphant eyes. Flo had brought him to the station to meet her when she came home. She had stood there in her black coat and ugly elaborate hat, holding onto him.

"You haven't congratulated us yet," she had said.

Janet had answered casually, "I haven't had time," and turned to her other friends. She hadn't even shaken hands with Alan, but she had seen his eyes. He was thinner and his eyes had lost their carefree assurance now.

They looked at her guiltily, guiltily, yes, and hungrily. That look haunted Janet. Long ago she had forgiven him. Now it hurt her to be looked at like this. "He'll soon get used to me," she thought.

But he didn't. Again and again as the days and evenings went on, Janet was to meet that look, from across a room filled with merrymakers, or darkly seen as she skated past him in the moonlight, her hand on someone's arm. Flo kept him always by her side, but she could not command his gaze.

Why should she think about him at all? Handsome as he

still was, Alan no longer wore the old air of golden youth. She knew him to be weak. She knew that he had chosen to marry an ugly and disagreeable girl so that he might be safe from the difficulties of having to make a living. She knew that he would always remain a boy, not having had the courage to become a man. And yet, having been in love with him, she could not now forget him. She pitied him and so long as she pitied him, the ghost of the old love held her.

Certainly, she made no attempt to see or speak with him. They never met save under Flo's watchful eye. No one who saw the three together—and for the first few weeks many watched eagerly—would have guessed that Alan had once meant anything to Janet. Her manner to them both was casual and indifferent, but many had noticed that whenever Janet was in the room, Alan's eyes followed her.

"Flo'd better look out," Annie Pratt voiced the general feeling of the crowd. "If she doesn't put Alan on a gold chain soon, she'll lose him."

Flo was taking no chances. She was vigilant at all times. And her talk was full of the things she and Alan were going to have after they were married.

"Alan's got his eyes on a pair of cream-colored horses. You never saw such beauties! Real high-steppers," she'd say, holding his arm possessively, or, "You ought to see the sailboat Alan's going to get when we're married. We went down to Lovell's to see it yesterday. It's almost finished; the best he's ever built, Ike says. Didn't he, Alan?"

Flo was a little pathetic these days, but the pathos was lost in a flood of ill-natured talk. She was always making slighting remarks about Janet and the Pierces in general. She breathed suspicion, uneasiness and ugliness of spirit wherever she went, like the witch's daughter, who lived east of the sun and west of the moon and was betrothed to the prince who was powerless against her, until his own true love came and broke the spell.

So matters went on all winter until one evening in late March when Alan and Janet found themselves at the same supper party at Susan Mann's. Alex was not there that evening as he had to work late at the store three nights a week. Flo had arrived with a red nose and such a cold that finally even she gave up and went home. Alan dutifully saw her back to her house and she had kept him until she thought the party would have broken up and everyone gone home; but he appeared just as the crowd was getting into their coats.

"Hi, Alan!" someone called. "We're all going smelt fishing tomorrow night at Tanner's brook. If this warm weather keeps up, they should be running in about an hour after the turn of the tide. We ought to meet by the road round ten-thirty, whoever's not afraid of getting their feet cold."

"Flo won't be able to come." Alan hesitated.

"You'd better take a night off."

Janet went by, wearing her red cloak.

"I'm seeing you home," Alan said loudly.

Janet drew in her breath, looking frightened for a moment. Then she smiled, almost naturally.

"That will be nice, Alan."

Sam Gildersleeve whistled when the door had closed behind them.

"What will Flo say to *that?*" he asked rhetorically.

"Did you ever see such a handsome couple?" murmured one of the girls.

It was little, plain-speaking Annie Pratt who expressed the more common feeling. "Jan's much too good for him even to see home, after the way he's acted!"

But that evening Alan *was* seeing Janet home again and for once, there was no hand pulling at his arm.

For awhile, they walked on in silence; then he burst out, "I wish it could always be like this!"

After a moment's silence, she asked, "What do you mean?"

He tried to take her hand but she kept it under her cloak.

"It was all a mistake. I was lonely. I didn't think your father would ever let you marry me and Flo never left me alone for a minute. Since you've come back, I've nearly gone crazy."

"But I would have married you, whatever Father said."

Alan said eagerly, "Your father seems much more friendly. He stopped me the other day and talked for quite a long time. He asked me how I was liking my job at the bank. You don't suppose he's changed his mind about me?"

Janet hesitated and then at last said uncertainly: "Father doesn't often change his mind. But if you're working, couldn't you support a wife?"

"I couldn't support myself even. It isn't much of a job, just kind of running errands. But I get out early in the afternoon and it sounds good to be working at a bank."

"But if you married me, you'd lose your job?"

"I suppose so," Alan agreed sullenly. "She'd see to that."

They walked along in silence and now they had come to the flagpole and the narrow common. In five minutes they would be home. The branches of the maples overhead were just coming into bud and they could see the stars through them.

Alan stopped and Janet stopped with him.

"Jan," he burst out, "I can't go on. Let's get married, whatever your father and Flo do. Please, Jan, forgive me. I know I haven't behaved well but I do love you, really and truly."

Janet felt the strength drain out of her, and her knees weakened so that she could scarcely stand. She tried to speak but could not. Her hands clenched and twisted together. But in the darkness Alan noticed nothing, and in a few moments Janet had regained her self-control.

"I forgave you long ago," she said steadily. "I always understood, and I'll go with you tonight, if you want me to."

He tried to kiss her but she wouldn't let him.

"Until we're married, you belong to Flo. I'll go in and get a few things ready. It isn't late and the family will still be up, but by midnight Father will be asleep. Come under my window then, and I'll come down."

Again he tried to kiss her, but again she pushed him away gently with hands whose trembling he was too excited to notice.

"Two hours," she said with a curious sadness, "and then you can kiss me as much as you like."

She was very different from the other impulsive Janet he had known. Alan was a little afraid of her quietness and of the things she didn't say; but still he wanted her.

At the door she turned to wave. He saw her outlined, dark on the light of the hallway; even her burning hair was dark. Then, almost with an effort, her fingers went to her mouth and she blew him a kiss before the door closed.

For Alan Loring, the hands of the clock had been turned back almost two years and once again he was offered his chance for happiness.

CHAPTER XXIV

Smelting by Moonlight

THERE was a cloud across the moon, black and edged with white fire. It seemed scarcely to stir in the motionless air and so it was the moon, rather, which slowly and radiantly climbed above the cloud. Janet sat by the open window waiting very quietly. The night air was cold and she had left on her cloak, but her hands, held tightly in her lap, were icy.

Sitting there, her eyes on the light in Alan's room, she heard after awhile the sounds of her father and mother coming upstairs and the closing of their door. Later, a buggy went by on the street with a comfortable clip-clop of unhurried hoofs and the lighter rustle of the wheels, and much later, the light in Alan's room went out.

What was he thinking? What was he doing now? Was it midnight yet? But she seemed unable to strike a match to look at her watch. She was caught up in a trance of waiting. Would the Loring back door open soon? Would she see him as a dark erect figure on his way to the stable to harness the horse? When Alan came, she would run downstairs and bring him in by the front door, call her father and mother, and announce their engagement. They would be married in church before all Thomaston.

But not unless he cared enough for her to choose a runaway marriage with her rather than Flo and her money. Surely he must show that he loved her enough to do that.

A light appeared in the darkness downstairs at the Lorings'. Someone turned up the gas in the lower hall. Surely it was Alan. A dim light appeared in the kitchen, remained for a few minutes and went out. On any other night, she would have guessed that he might be raiding the icebox, but tonight he was getting ready. Soon the door would open.

Scarcely moving, scarcely breathing, cold hands tightly clasped, Janet waited. The light in the hall went out. Then nothing further happened. The moon rose high above the treetops, bright in a cloudless blue of heaven. At last, when she was so stiff that she could scarcely get to her feet, Janet went to her dressing table, struck a match, and looked at her watch.

It was fourteen minutes past one.

She felt the little fire of the match hot against her fingers and blew it out. Then in the darkness she undressed, but it was a long, long time before she went to sleep.

At half past ten the next evening, the moon, delaying, had not yet risen when the crowd gathered on the road above Tanner's brook. Susan Mann and Alex Hunt and a tired Janet had driven over in Perley Snow's father's carryall, with five or six others all crowded in together. Flo's cold was worse and Alan had stayed home as everyone thought he would. But Steve and Millard and two or three younger boys had come on bicycles, and so had the Driscoll girls with Mr. Driscoll. Everyone brought bushel baskets and lanterns turned down low.

Giggling and stumbling and exclaiming under their breaths, they crossed the hayfield single file to where the brook ran down among coarse grasses. The young men cautiously shone their lanterns on the water. The fish had not come yet. Spreading lap robes on the grass, the young people waited, rubbing their mittened hands, whispering together, exploding into stifled gasps of laughter, exclaiming "Hush!"

Suddenly, a voice said, "They're coming," and everyone listened.

Along the brook there came a faint rustling sound, as the close-packed school of smelt made its way up between the grassy banks. Here and there, a fish tail splashed faintly in the shallows. The sound approached, a little like the stirring of branches as a wind comes through a wood. Now it was abreast where the young people waited; now it was past.

"Let them get well up," Perley Snow said in a low voice. "Last time we went in too soon and they turned back."

Everyone was busy taking off shoes and stockings and getting ready the baskets.

"Now," said Perley Snow.

Alex pulled Janet to her feet and together they waded into the brook. The dark water was swift and shallow and icily cold. It was alive with fish, cold bodies sliding past their legs, going upstream, in an almost solid mass. All along the bank, young people were stepping into the brook, restraining their cries as the chill current of water and the counter-tide of smelt struck against their bare legs. The girls had their skirts pinned up a little below their knees, and the dull light of the lanterns on the bank shone on the tin pails, which everyone carried in their left hands, leaving their right hands free for catching smelts, for in this fishing no nets were allowed.

Now the catch had begun. Everyone was seizing upon the slippery bodies with their right hands, and the pails echoed with the flapping of fish. The night air had an underwater smell, the faintly clammy odor of live smelt.

Janet's pail was nearly full.

"I'll have to take it back to the basket," she said to Alex in a low voice.

"Let me take it for you," he offered. It was the first time he had spoken to her since he had helped her down the bank.

They had both been very silent that evening.

After twenty minutes, Perley lighted a bonfire back from the bank, and the fishers came out to warm their frozen feet and hands.

"They won't turn back now," Perley declared. "Anyway, we have nearly all we want."

"Speak for yourself," said one of the boys. "Ma told me she wanted three bushels for pickling."

Everyone wanted more. Perhaps of all the crowd, only Janet would have been glad not to put her hand down into the water again to bring out another unseen eight-inch creature silently struggling for its poor anonymous life. She was sad under all the excitement and gaiety with which she was surrounded, and Alex was either sad or angry about something, for he had scarcely spoken at all. As Janet rubbed her cold feet with her hands, she made an effort and tried several times to talk to him, but Alex, usually so cheerful, let the conversation die each time.

The fire flared up, sending its tongues of red flame towards the stars, and Millard, seeing Janet's face, rosy in the light, was suddenly struck by its expression. Out of the corner of his eye, he watched her and Alex Hunt and then unobtrusively drew Stephen from the circle.

"Hey, Steve, something's wrong with Janet and Alex."

[193]

"Ouch." Steve had stubbed his toe on a stone. "You're imagining things. He's around our house a lot."

"But tonight he's mad about something. He won't talk to her."

Steve became more interested.

"Lovers' quarrel, I guess. I had a row with Loantha the other day, myself."

Millard's feeling for Janet was touched with a boy's romanticism.

"We ought to do something to help."

Steve was not interested. "Rot," he said matter-of-factly. "My feet are ready to drop off with cold. Janet can take care of herself." And he sought the fire.

But Millard didn't think so. A beautiful girl needed help, and he, as a man—well, almost a man, anyhow—must come to her rescue one way or another. The crowd was singing, and while they sang in the shadows, the living tide of fish pushed its way up and up the brook, and Millard watched Janet and Alex and meditated.

"All right!" said Perley, "Back to fishing," and the young men helped the girls to their feet.

"In the sky the bright stars glittered," someone led off.

"On the bank the pale moon shone," the other voices took up the singing. "And 'twas from Aunt Dinah's quilting party (Horrors! Its colder than ever!) I was seeing Nellie (Ouch!) home." They were all singing now, as the smelting began again— ("What a whopper!")

"I was seeing Nellie home, I was seeing Nellie home, And 'twas from Aunt Dinah's quilting party, I was seeing Nellie home."

Somehow Janet and Alex must be alone for awhile. Perhaps the song gave Millard the idea. Perhaps, born of a mixture of adolescent chivalry and adolescent roughhousing, the idea would have occurred to him anyway. For the last time, he tried the boy's way of setting the world to rights by means subtle enough in intent, but direct in application.

As Janet stepped once more into the stream, helped in silence by Alex, Millard took his place behind her. Before she had really got her footing, he slipped and fell against her, throwing her off balance so that she went down on her knees into the brook. Instantly Alex and Millard, who was apologizing vehemently, pulled her to her feet again. Her skirts were wet and bedraggled, but, fortunately, her bodice and short coat were still dry.

"You'd better stand by the fire," Alex suggested indifferently, as some of the others left their fishing and appeared at the scene; but this was no part of Millard's plan.

"And catch her death of cold, like Flo?" he scoffed. "She ought to go straight home and change her things. I'm awfully sorry, Jan. You'll have to let Alex take you home in Perley's rig; he'll be back in time to collect the rest of us."

"Sure," said Perley, "but you come right on back, Alex."

Susan Mann drew Janet aside into the shadows.

"I'll lend you my flannel petticoat and you'd better take off all that wet stuff. You can wrap yourself in one of the robes. Thank goodness, your shoes and stockings will be dry."

When Janet climbed into the carryall beside Alex, she was informally dressed, but quite comfortable, if a little bespattered and damp around the wrists. Her basket of fish and a bundle of wet skirts were put on the floor behind them, the horse was untied and off they started. For awhile, they drove on in silence. At last, Alex said in a tight voice, "Did Alan Loring walk home with you last night?"

"Yes."

"So I heard."

For awhile, there was again silence except for the sound of the hoof beats and the creaking of the carriage. Then Janet said painfully, "I agreed to run away with him."

The horse jumped forward into a gallop under a sudden descent of the whip and had to be pulled down again.

"You *what?*"

"But he never came."

"Jan, what do you mean?"

She was shivering now, but he refused to notice it.

"He asked me and I said 'Yes.' I didn't tell him that Father had said he wouldn't disown me after all. If he wanted me more than Flo's money, I'd marry him. I couldn't see him ruining his life without trying to help him. I told you that on the train."

Her voice was pleading but the young man was not moved by it.

"So you let him jilt you a second time."

She shivered and went on.

"If he had come, I'd have done my best to make him a good wife. It wasn't for my sake but for his. Please try to understand, Alex."

Her teeth were chattering so hard that even in his anger, he was forced to notice it.

"Wrap yourself up; we'll soon be home." But he couldn't leave the subject. "When he didn't come, how did you feel?"

"I felt glad, of course."

"Glad? In Heaven's name, what for?" he exploded, and the horse started forward again.

Alex could scarcely hear her answer.

"Because now I'm free of him. He's made his choice and I don't have to worry any more about him. I can do as I please."

He tried to see her face in the dusk.

"One of us is crazy." But his voice had changed.

Suddenly the tension broke and he had his arms around her and her arms were around him.

"Is that what you wanted, Jan?" he asked, before he kissed her.

"I knew even on the train," she whispered, between chattering teeth.

Yet in his arms she was soon warm again. The moon, which had delayed, now showed itself over the distant river, without a cloud to blemish its spring silver, and the peepers were ringing their thousand bells from a hollow. The horse slowed down from a trot to a walk and at last came to a halt and began to tear at the new short grass by the side of the road, moving forward a step or two at a time, pulling the wheels out of the spring ruts with a jolt. But no one noticed or at least no one cared.

After awhile, they remembered the others.

"I suppose we ought to go back for them," he said.

"I suppose so."

"They'll wonder why I didn't take you home."

"Tell them, then."

With a kind easy hand, Alex pulled the horse's head up from the grass and turned the creature about. The front wheels rasped and cramped, the carryall tipped; they jolted back into position and then were off, trotting towards Tanner's brook, the horse going unwillingly now, since it was going away from its stable.

They were driving straight into the moon. Alex looked at Janet's face. How often he had watched her, ever since she was a girl at school with two braids down her back, but he had never before seen her look like this. Perhaps only once in a lifetime is a person completely happy. Far-off, red under the white moon, they could see the fire beside the brook and the shadowy waiting figures of their friends, and scarcely as loud as the sound of the peepers, came the distant singing.

It was an old song which they had all been practicing that winter at singing school, and now the harmony rose faint and sweet over the fields and copses, so still and bright in the moonlight that even the grass and buds seemed made of silver metal.

"Where-e'er you tread the blushing flowers shall rise,
And all things flourish, and all things flourish
Where'er you turn your eyes."

The young men's voices blended with the girls', and like a promise, the song came across the tranquil countryside to greet them.